THE QUANTUM CYPHER

By SRIRAM B.

DISCLAIMER

This is a work of fiction. Names, characters, businesses, places, events and incidents are either the products of the author's imagination or used in a fictitious manner. Any resemblance to actual persons, living or dead, or actual events is purely coincidental.

230 B.C.

The caravan slowly moved through the mountainous terrain, only two of the twelve-member team were still alive. Dressed in heavy body armour, they got off their horses and started to unload what appeared to be wooden boxes. Both men never spoke but worked in unison to drop the boxes into the steep crevice. After they had disposed of the boxes, the men cut the horses free, quietly embraced each other and parted ways

---

CHAPTER 1

Present Day

"Everything ok?" asked Cara, looking at the worried face of her husband, Andrew (Andy to his friends and family).

"Nothing to worry, I'm just looking for my car keys," he replied.

"It must be at the key holder," said Eric, an eight-year-old with the attitude of a teenager. "I checked, it is not there," said Andy scratching his stubble, a sure sign of a holiday.

"Got it," shouted Ava, a ten-year-old diva from the next room. "It was on the dining table."

"Great! While I step out to get earphones for the trip, you can finish your packing. Hong Kong, here we come," shreiked Andy in excitement.

"Don't get too excited dad, it's an eight-hour flight with a two hour layover in Kuala Lumpur. It's going to be another marathon?" said Ava resignedly.

"I promise this time it will be different," laughed Andy.

Walking down the memory lane, he could still feel the anxiety of their last holiday to Italy. Cara had booked their return on a crazy schedule. It was 22-hour marathon starting from Marilleva, a ski resort in the Alps. First, it was a bus journey to Trento, then a train to Venice. Next it was a boat ride from Venice to the mainland, another bus ride to the airport, then took a flight to Rome, where they boarded a flight back to Dubai. They had covered all modes of transportation in a single day.

After the vacation to Italy, the kids refused to travel on a tight schedule and demanded a relaxing holiday.

"Are you carrying tickets, passport and credit cards? Hope you have exchanged the currency?" enquired Cara.
"Everything is done. I have even double checked our reservation at the hotel and have arranged for airport pickup."
"That's surprising," added Eric.
"His productivity level peaks only during holidays, after which he will be back to himself," Ava offered her expert analysis.
"Yes, the absent-minded professor," laughed Cara.

Andrew had a poor working memory. Although, he had a good long term memory. During his school days in London, he found it difficult to memorise his course work. His father encouraged him to write down tasks and to-do lists. Ever since, he always carried a memo pad with him and was known among friends and family as the "Memo Man".

He held a Master's degree in History due to his interest in culture, but never pursued it. He always dreamt of travelling the world to explore new cultures and people.

During the INTERNET boom, he got onto the IT bandwagon and became a programmer. Later in his career, he moved to Dubai and currently worked as an IT Business Development Manager.

Cara, on the other hand, was a very sensible person. She holds a Master's degree in Science. She was very hardworking and disciplined. Although being poles apart, it was love at first sight when Andy met her during a college cultural festival. Three months later, he proposed to her on the steps of the university library and the rest, as they say, is history.

"The taxi is here! Time to go," called out Andy. "Double check all the power switches and make sure that they are off and please check the AC in every room."

"Checked, and ok," replied Cara.

The taxi sped towards Dubai International Airport. Dubai is a multicultural and diverse city. It is bustling with people from all around the world and is known for its shopping arcades.
Over the years, Dubai has become one of the leading cities in the world due to its visionary leaders.

The taxi came to a halt at the Departure gate of the Dubai International Airport. The driver was kind to help them with the luggage.
"Counter number 22," informed Cara looking at the flight departure monitor.
"Passengers for Hong Kong, this way please," directed the customer service clerk.

After Immigration and security clearance, 20 minutes later they boarded the flight and were ready to take off.
Andy settled into his seat and closed his eyes and looked forward to a great holiday.

CHAPTER 2

As the aircraft began to descend, Andy looks at the landscape and the tall skyscrapers that seem to touch the sky.
The weather was hot and humid, 37 degrees centigrade with a clear sky. The pilot gently manoeuvres the aircraft on touchdown towards the docking gate.

Ava nudges Eric, who is fast asleep. Waking up disoriented "have we landed?" he asks rubbing his eyes. "Yes, we have," replied Andy.
The Hong Kong Airport is a located on an island, and it can be reached from the mainland by road through the Tsing Ma Bridge, a 2.2 km long connection between Hong Kong International Airport (Lantau Island) and Hong Kong Kowloon City side. It's vibrant; the densely populated urban centre is a major port and global financial hub with a skyscraper-studded skyline.

Walking out of the Hong Kong Airport, Andy looks at the hundreds of taxi and transport drivers holding the names of customers, at the end of the line he finds a board with his name on it. A short man in his late forties wearing the hotel uniform smiles and hesitantly calls out "Mr Andrew Clarke?" Andy hands him the hotel booking receipt.

"Welcome to Hong Kong. I am Yang, the Hotel driver. If you need to go anywhere in Hong Kong, you can call me directly" he says, handing over his phone number scribbled on a piece of paper. "The hotel also offers shuttle service to the airport and the nearest metro station every 30 minutes. Additionally, the bus stop is just 5 minutes from the hotel."

"That's great! Are there any good restaurants near the hotel?" asked Cara.

Yang was eager to share his knowledge of the city. "Yes, Madam, we have a couple of fast food restaurants and a 24/7 grocery store just opposite the hotel. The hotel also offers room service. The food from the hotel restaurant is also excellent and is not very expensive."

"Thanks for the information, we will keep that in mind," said Cara.

The taxi crawled through Hong Kong's busy streets, "Is this your first time here, Sir?" Enquired Yang, while passing by the port where large Cruise ships were anchored close to the Victoria Bay.
"Yes, " answered Andy looking out of the window. What are the must-see tourist attractions in Hong Kong? Asked Cara. Yang quickly digs into the dashboard and hands over a tourist guide with the map of Hong Kong. "My brother runs a taxi service for visitors and one can hire his services for a day to take you anywhere in Hong Kong for only 200 Hong Kong dollars." Thanks for that Yang. We have already purchased tickets for the Bus tour and Metro pass, we will let you know if we need to go to a place where the service is not available." informed Cara politely.

Vstar Hotel was a beautiful 4-star property located in Central Hong Kong. The metro and bus stop was close by, just as Yang had indicated. The staff were friendly and directed them to their two-bedroom suite.

Eric rushed into his room and immediately opened the balcony door. Stepping into a clean and chic balcony, he looked at the landscape in front of him and exclaimed, "It's beautiful!."

"That is the Victoria Harbour," the bellboy pointed out. "In the evening, you can see many ships that dock out there. Cruise ships travelling these waters usually start from Singapore, but you can often spot ships from Japan and Australia too."

"Look at what we have here," said Andy pointing to the kitchen.

"I'm not going anywhere close to that place," said Cara, trying hard to keep the kids from fighting over their choice of bed.

Andy pulls out a bottle of sparkling wine from the mini bar.
"What about us?" asked Eric coyly, hinting at the cola inside the fridge.

"There is a cold bottle of water for you," joked Andy inviting a pounce from Eric.
"You are such a baby," said Cara, running her hands through Eric's hair.

"What about me?" cribbed Ava. "He gets all the attention just because he is good in academics."

"Come on now cheer up. You are the best girl in the universe, and as I always tell everyone, you are the best thing that has happened to me," pacified Andy.

Cara rolls her eyes, pulls out a pack of Orange juice from the pantry and hands it over to the kids. The family cuddles over by the window and enjoy the sunset over the beautiful skyline of Hong Kong.

CHAPTER 3

Andy woke up and reached for his bedside clock it was 8:30 in the morning. Cara was fast asleep next to him, he stretched himself and got out of bed. Walking over to the kid's room, he found Eric looking out of the window. "Good morning," whispered Andy hugging Eric. "You're up early."

"Yes, I was freezing and couldn't sleep. Ava had lowered the AC temperature last night. So what's for breakfast?" Eric asked. Andy hatched a plan, "Let's have a quick shower and head over to the hotel restaurant. The ladies can order room service once they wake up."
"Good Idea" quipped Eric, and they set out to start their day.

An hour later, when Andy and Eric returned to the room after a sumptuous breakfast, they found mum and daughter still in a state of deep slumber. Eric looked at his dad and quipped "Unbelievable, we are going to waste the entire day sitting in the hotel."

"Don't worry. I'll wake them up in a jiffy." said Andy, opening the curtains and letting the bright sunlight into the room.
"I'll get some water to splash on them," said Eric excitedly. Eric was ambushed and found a wall of water hitting his face. Completely surprised he turned around to look at Andy,
"It's not me," he said, pointing to Cara, who was sitting on the bed with a bottle of water in her hand.

"The joke's on you, " she laughed. Eric pounced on her, and both were fake wrestling. Hearing this commotion, Ava yelled "What's happening?" from the other room. "Your dad and brother got a nasty surprise," replied Cara.

"C'mon girls. We are running late. Get dressed and let's head out to explore Hong Kong. First stop is at Victoria Peak," said Andy.

Victoria Peak is a mountain in the western half of Hong Kong Island.
It is a major tourist attraction that offers views over Central Hong Kong and Victoria Harbour. They had a fabulous and tiring day.

Returning to the hotel room in the evening, Andy's crashed into the bed for a quick nap before heading for Dinner. They headed downtown to visit the famous Harbour Mall on Canton Road. The mall had a cruise terminal and restaurants serving international cuisine. They visited a famous Thai restaurant and savoured some of their signature dishes.

Next morning, Andy was surprised, as he was the last one to wake up. It must have been the sake, a traditional sweet, low-alcoholic Japanese drink made from fermented rice.
"Wake up lazy bones," whispered Cara pecking him on the cheek.
"Want some water treatment dad?" Yelled Eric walking over to the window.
The troop was up and about in the morning. It was a unanimous decision not to have breakfast at the hotel restaurant as they wanted to try something new. Andy was ready in 20 minutes, and they left the hotel for the day-two adventure.

Grabbing a sandwich at a cafe nearby, Andy spoke about the day's plan. "First, we visit the Temple on

the southern side of Lion Rock in the north of
Kowloon and then top it with a ferry ride through
Victoria Harbour.
"Boring" snarled Eric. "I want to visit Disneyland
and Ocean Park.
 "I am with him," said Eva.
"Sorry Kiddos, it's already been booked for tomorrow
and the day after," said Andy.

So, they set out as per plan to Kowloon. A 45-minute
ride in a metro and a few minutes of walk through the
busy markets of Kowloon brought them to the door
of the Buddhist Temple.

Andy stood mesmerised by the beauty of the temple
and its surroundings. The temple was nestled right in
the middle of the busy business district of Hong
Kong, yet a peaceful oasis. The sweet smell of
incense caught his attention, and as he turned,
bumped into a monk who was carrying the incense
sticks.
"I'm sorry," said Andy, "Please accept my apology."
 The Monk smiled at him and said, " Nei Hou" in
Chinese. Realising Andy was a visitor, he quickly
turned to English. "You have come a long way from
home".
"Yes," said Andy, "We are from Dubai," Pointing to
his family.

"How do you like the temple," Inquired the monk
with an Indian accent.
 "The architecture is beautiful and the sense of peace,
the minute you enter the temple is amazing," said
Andy.
 "It was created for worship and a place of
meditation. The design and architecture have been

built by the monastery to enable a person to enter into a state of self-reflection," said the Monk.

"How long are you here for," he asked. "Just for a week," said Andy. "That's a pity you should take the time to discover yourself by spending time at the monastery, maybe the next time around?"

"Yes, most definitely," said Andy, having no idea what the Monk meant. Smiling, he handed Andy an incense stick, pointing towards the place where thousands of incense sticks were already lit by other devotees. As Andy turned to leave, the Monk placed his hand on his shoulder and whispered, "You will become the sales director for your company before your next birthday, good luck and all the very best."

CHAPTER 4

"Dad" shouted Eric, dazed and confused at what the monk had just told him, Andy turned to see Eric who was holding his leg in pain. He had locked his leg into the railings trying to get a glimpse of the fish pond. Andy ran over and slowly released Eric's leg from the railing. Slightly bruised, he was crying in pain. The monk immediately led them to his office. It was a large room with a table in the corner. In the middle, there was a meditation mat and an old book which was spread out on the floor, mantras thought Andy. "Thank you, sir," said Andy. "Call me Ginko," said the monk smiling at Eric.
"You will be fine in just a moment." Leading him over to a tap used to wash your legs and hands before entering the main hall. Ginko washed Eric's legs gently and told him there was nothing to be worried as the water had healing properties. "The bruises should be healed in no time," he quipped.
Just when Andy thought to question him about his prophecy, Ginko's mobile phone started ringing. "Excuse me," he kindly said and spoken in a foreign tongue that Andy could not recognise. "Apologising for not being able to spend more time due to more pressing matters. Enjoy your stay," he waved and walked into the main hall.
Andy stood deep in thought when he felt someone pulling at his shirt. Whirling around, he found Eric, who was waving his hand before his face.
 "Where are you, come back to earth, " he giggled. "Look at my leg, the bruises have disappeared," he said.
 Andy reached out for Erick's leg to get a closer look. He was right. There were no signs of any bruising. "Do you feel any pain?"

"Nope, nothing at all." Rubbing the bruised area, he whispered, "Can't even feel any pain when I press on it. That's amazing. Get a bottle dad, we need to take as much as water from the tap as we can. I want to tell mum and Ava about this."

That's strange, thought Andy. Me, a sales director in 2 months, October 10th being my birthday? It's impossible.

Andy worked for an IT company based in Dubai owned by the Kareem family. The unit was headed by their youngest son Omar. He had visited Dubai 20 years ago and had instantly fallen in love with the region and prospects for business. Despite a lot of opposition from his family in Morocco he left and started a trading company in Dubai. Over the years, he expanded into multiple industries and successfully build a conglomerate of companies. Andy worked for the IT solutions firm. Omar believed in being close to his employees and always had an open-door policy. He directly participated in the running of all the companies, but had employed Directors for each of the units. Tony Campbell, the current Sales and Marketing Director, was Andy's Boss. He was a successful IT Professional from London and had worked with many of the top IT firms before joining Omar. The story goes that Tony had bumped into Omar during one of the conferences in London and after a few emails appointed him to lead the sales team in Dubai. Given his experience, it seemed impossible that he will be given the position of Director in a matter of 2 months, especially when there are no signs of trouble. Even if Tony was switching jobs, Directors had a three month notice period and from Andy's knowledge, Tony had not resigned or was asked to put down his papers. So the whole prophecy of becoming the IT Director in 2 months seemed impossible. Andy moved on to explore the rest of the temple, as he was gazing at the Buddha statue when he felt Cara's hand holding his arm.

"Beautiful, isn't it?" She whispered.

"Yes, it must have taken them years to carve this statue out of a single stone, not to mention the intricate colouring and the fact that it has not faded being exposed to the elements is amazing.

"Maybe it was painted recently," she uttered.

"I heard of Eric's magical healing session. He has been begging me to fill up the water bottles with the water from the tap there," she pointed, where he was with Ava filling up his water bottle.

CHAPTER 5

"Still thinking about what happened?" asked Cara, looking at Andy, who was gazing out of the train window deep in thought.

"Yep. What's surprising is the fact that, he said 'Sales Director'. How did he know that? I never told him anything about my profession and he also said you are far from home.

"Okay, now that could be just a generic statement considering we are all tourists. You really don't have to put yourself through this. He must have confused you with someone else.

"I doubt it," said Andy.

"He was quite certain and there was a mischievous look in his face as he knew that I would take him seriously and ponder over it. Then you should have seen the way he cured Eric's leg the bruises just disappeared in 5 minutes and believe me, they were no minor scratches. He just wiped it with water. He said the water had healing powers. But it's one thing to hear another to see it for yourself."

"So, what do you plan to do about it?" Cara sighed impatiently.

"Its 2 months away, and if it does turn out the way he predicted. Congrats! Let's party!"

"I guess you are right. No point in dwelling on it, but the experience is very intriguing and has made me curious."

"Come now, we have a holiday to enjoy," said Cara, "And we need to get off at the next stop to see the Po Lin Monastery. The place is supposed to be beautiful and has a vegetarian restaurant where we can grab lunch."

"Oh no, another Temple," cribbed the kids. "Can't wait for tomorrow. I am looking forward to Disney

Land and guess what? I get to buy a toy of my
choice."
 "Yeah, right! Andy smiled, "Here we go again. At
this rate, we will need an extra suitcase to take all the
stuff you guys purchased."
Po Lin Monastery is a Buddhist monastery, located
on Ngong Ping Plateau, on Lantau Island, Hong
Kong.
The monastery was founded in 1906 by three monks
visiting from Jiangsu Province on the Chinese
mainland and was initially known simply as,'The Big
Hut'. It was renamed to its present name in 1924. The
main temple houses three bronze statues of the
Buddha – representing his past, present and future
lives – as well as many Buddhist scriptures.
The restaurant inside the monastery served fresh
vegetarian food that lived up to the family's
expectations and they topped it with green tea. Back
at the hotel room Andy ordered a bottle of Sake and
looked out at the beautiful view of Victoria Harbour
when suddenly he had a vision of sitting in a pool of
blood holding a sword.
Why am I getting such a gruesome image? he
wondered, looking at the night sky from his window.
"Start packing everything you need for the Disney
Land trip," cooed Cara. "It's a long way from here
and we must take the shuttle in the morning to the
train station at 5:30 A.M., so hit the bed everyone,
that goes for you too, 'Mr. Sake'.

CHAPTER 6

Sitting by a pool of blood the figure stares down at the sword lost in thought. His armour was made of metal and his hands were covered in blood, but he showed no signs of being aware of where he was as the sun was about to set and then he heard the clank of metal. Turning around, he saw an axe being wielded at him.

Waking up with a sudden jolt and breaking into a sweat, Andy searched frantically for the light switch. Unable to find it, he grabbed his mobile phone. It was 2:35 A.M.

"What is going on?" hissed Cara. Being a light sleeper, she was always aware of any noise or disturbance during the night. Her brothers always depended on her to open the door when they would come home late after a night out with their friends.

"Just a nightmare," dismissed Andy. "What was it about?" Asked Cara.

"Can't remember. But I felt like there was some impending danger."

"You are sweating profusely. Maybe you should have another shot of Sake and sleep," said Cara.

Walking over to the window and looking at the beautiful view, Andy could see the activity in the Cruise ships with disco lights on the terrace. Lights from the minivans dropping off staff after their duty and taxis transporting tourist. Hong Kong is a city that never sleeps like many metros around the world. The influx of tourist and the sea port lead to a steady stream of activity. Opening a mini bottle of whisky and a packet of crisps Andy settled down on the couch, a couple of sips and he was fast asleep.

At 5:30 A.M., the alarm sounded and Andy slowly stirred on the couch to reach the alarm clock. I feel like being runover by a truck, let me have some strong coffee, he thought switching off the alarm on the phone, he softly shook Cara, "Don't go back to sleep. We have to go to Disneyland today and the kids are looking forward to it."

"I have just called the concierge and booked the taxi. It will be here in 45 minutes," informed Andy. Heading over to the kid's room, he switched on the lights and pulled the curtains open. The sun was yet to rise, but the activity on the streets was increasing as he could see people walking and jogging towards the seaside pathways.

Slipping into bed with Eric and Ava, he slowly whispered into their ears, "Wakey Wakey! It's Disneyland today!"
They jumped off the bed with excitement.
Ten minutes later, both kids had finished brushing their teeth and were off for a shower. Andy was wondering how he was going to get through the day sinking back into the couch for a few winks when a pillow came flying at him. Pulling him from the couch Cara ushered him into the toilet.
"You can sleep all you like when you get back," she grinned.
As Andy stared at the toilet mirror, he found a stain on his T-shirt. Removing his t-shirt, he examined it. Not whisky, it's too dark. Looking closely he realised, it was blood.

CHAPTER 7

Memories flooded back to his teenage years. Playing
football in the neighbourhood playground, he would
come home to suddenly find blood dripping from the
nose. He would tell his mum what happened and if
there was anything to be worried about. Nothing
serious, she would tell him,"It's just the heat and your
body is growing."
Watching his nose, Andy thought. It's been 15 years
since the bleeding had stopped. The AC temperature
was set to 21 degrees so it's not the heat. Must have
been the dream. I guess it was quite realistic.
Unfortunately, I don't remember anything except the
emotion of being in great danger, he thought.

The taxi was waiting by the reception door. It was a
45 minutes' drive through picturesque locales. The
Taxi stopped in front of the Disney station and the
kids got off and rushed over to the ticket counter.
They were looking forward to the day and finally it
was here.
Hong Kong Disneyland is a theme park located on
reclaimed land in Penny's Bay, Lantau Island. They
first visited the Mystic Manor, an old house with a
built-in carriageway taking one through the house.
Eric then ran over to the Jungle River Cruise, a ride
through the river surrounded by wild animals that had
Ava at her wit's end, when a hippopotamus rose out
of the river to open its mouth wide open. The
attractions looked so real that it can easily be
mistaken for the original. Toy Soldier Parachute
Drop followed next, where you are asked to sit in a
large parachute shaped seat that is lifted high into the
air. The ride was not scary but Eric loved the toy
story theme and took the ride three times in a row.
Bugged Ava pulled them over to the Festival of the

Lion King, a musical extravaganza of music and dance showcasing the Lion King story. It was almost sundown and there were so many rides still left to be experienced. Andy had left the best for last. The Big Grizzly Mountain Runaway Mine Cars, a ride not for the faint hearted. The mine cars sped through the mountain. The highlight of the ride caught Cara and Ava by surprise when the cars suddenly travelled in the reverse direction. The kids screamed in excitement and never wanted the day to end.

They visited the shops to pick up gifts and memorabilia for friends back home. At the end of a memorable and fun filled day was the most spectacular Disney firework show that dazzled the night sky. They managed to find a place in time for a magical show. Returning to the Disney station, which featured Mickey themed train with windows in the shape of Mickey's face.

CHAPTER 8

Catching the last train out of Disneyland, Andy's family found themselves waiting for the taxi. It was late and there were many people waiting for their turn. Finally, a taxi pulled over, but Andy decided not to take it. Cara looked at Andy in absolute amazement, "the kids are tired and it's late at night. What was that all about?" she demanded.
"I just didn't feel good," said Andy.
But luckily for him, another taxi pulled over. Andy quickly perched himself in the front seat and the kids along with Cara got onto the back. The taxis in Hong Kong were red in colour and had an antique look. However, the interiors and engine performance matched that of a modern saloon. As they were heading out, Cara pointed out to a taxi that they had ditched earlier. The driver stopped to enquire if they had a spare jack as the car had a flat tire. Glancing back, Andy saw Cara looking at him in amusement.
"So, you're a psychic now." She quipped.
Andy smiled and said, "Was just a lucky guess."
Getting back to the hotel room, Andy settled the kids into bed and walked over to the mini bar to grab the whisky.
"Do you need anything?" he asked, Cara. Maybe some red wine. Heading back to the mini bar, Andy picked up a fine bottle of red wine from Italy.
"So, what's the plan for tomorrow?" asked, Cara.
"You look tired," she said. "Let's take it easy tomorrow and shop around. Hong Kong is known for the busy shopping areas and one can find anything under the sun."
Andy woke up to find Eric staring at him, "That's a surprise. You are up early."
"I could not sleep as the room was very cold," said Eric.

"Give me 10 minutes. I will have a quick wash and then we can head over to the restaurant for breakfast."
"No way Dad, they serve the same food every day. So let's go somewhere else."
"That reminds me, where are mum and Eva?"
"They have gone to the swimming pool and will take some time to come."
"In that case, let's both step out for breakfast. I know you don't like the food, but I promise to take you to a great place for lunch."
Just as there were picking up the breakfast, Eric looked at Andy in panic.
"Your nose is bleeding. I'll call mum."
"Just relax, it is a condition I have had since childhood." Andy went on to explain how he had this condition and what his mum used to say to him.
"So, I guess you are still growing up," giggled Eric. Returning to the room, they found the ladies back from their swim. Eric quickly updated them on what had transpired during breakfast.
"You did not have this problem for over 15 years. Wonder what caused it?" enquired Cara. "It's the second time this has happened after I've come to Hong Kong. But I don't think there's anything to worry. Let's go out and have some fun shopping," urged Andy.
It was a beautiful day and the family enjoyed their walk to the metro station. As they were boarding the train, Andy felt a tug on his pants. Running his hand down into the pant pockets he realised that the wallet was missing.

CHAPTER 9

Horrified at the thought of being stuck without any money, credit cards and the long-drawn process of applying for duplicate documents made Andy break into a sweat. It was just the start of their vacation and being out of the country only made things worse. Looking at his face, Cara realised that something was wrong, "Are you ok?"

"Someone stole my wallet as I was getting into the train," panicked Andy.

"Oh no. What will we do for lunch," said Eric with a horrified look!

Andy could not stop himself from laughing.

"I have lost my wallet and all you can think of is lunch?"

"I am sure he will faint if you tell him there is no lunch," added Eva.

"Don't worry guys. I have my credit card in my purse with some cash" said, Cara.

"We can manage, thank God," grinned Eric.

"Let's get off at the next station and place a complaint with the police."

10 minutes later, Andy was explaining what had happened to a police officer who listened intently and took notes. He asked them where they were staying and when they plan to leave. He led them into his office and lodged a complaint on a computer. "Do you have a local cell phone number where I can reach you?" "No, don't have one. But if you call the hotel and leave a message, I will call back," said Andy.

"As a precaution, please inform the banks that you have lost your cards as things could get out of hand very fast. Especially, if the perpetrator starts to use your credit cards online."

"So, what you want to do now," asked Cara.

"Do you want to go back to the hotel and relax or do
we stick with the plan?"
"Let's stick with the plan," said Andy. "The cards all
have a pin number. So nothing to worry about and
there's really nothing much that we can do now
except wait. So let's not waste the day. I will call the
hotel and inform them as the hotel key was in my
wallet. I will also request for a duplicate key.
Anything of value in your bags and suitcase?"
"Yes. I have left some jewellery in the room" replied
Cara. Getting off the phone, Andy guided the family
into the train to Tian Tan Buddha, also known as the
Big Buddha, is a large bronze statue of Buddha
Shakyamuni, completed in 1993, and located at
Ngong Ping, Lantau Island, in Hong Kong. The
statue is sited near Po Lin Monastery and symbolises
the harmonious relationship between man and nature,
people and faith. It is a major centre of Buddhism in
Hong Kong and is also a popular tourist attraction.
Getting off the train the Andys took the Ngong Ping
Cable Car, a 5.7-kilometre (3.5 mi) long bi-cable
gondola lift system (referred to by its operators as a
"cable car") linking between Tung Chung (where it
connects the MTR Tung Chung station) and Ngong
Ping (where the Po Lin Monastery and Tian Tan
Buddha are located). The cable car journey offers a
25-minute aerial alternative to the current one-hour
journey by Tung Chung Road, allowing visitors to
glide across Tung Chung Bay and up to Lantau Island
towards Ngong Ping Plateau. Getting off the cable
car, the family visited the Ngong Ping Village. Built
next to the Ngong Ping Cable Car Terminal, occupies
a 15,000 square metre site and has been designed to
mirror and uphold the cultural and spiritual veracity
of the Ngong Ping area. Traditional Chinese
architectural designs are a feature of the Ngong Ping
Village, which contains an assortment of shopping

and dining experiences. They also visited a number of key attractions including Walking with Buddha, the Monkey's Tale Theatre and the Ngong Ping Tea House.

CHAPTER 10

"It's 10 P.M.," said Andy, getting off the metro station. "We were lucky to get the last train back to Hong Kong."

Walking into the Hotel, they headed over to the reception area and told the clerk about the lost key card. A couple of minutes later, the front office manager said the request has been handled and the key was changed. A key card lock, he explained, is a lock operated by a key card, a flat, rectangular plastic card with identical dimensions to that of a credit card or driver's license, which stores a physical or digital signature which the door mechanism accepts before disengaging the lock.

He handed over the key card and bid farewell. On entering the room Cara shouted out loud, "STOP! Someone has been in the room."

Stepping into the room, she found nothing unusual. Andy looked at Cara and she pointed to the writing table. Andy's wallet was on the table with a note. Picking it up cautiously, he read, "Sorry for the trouble. Don't tell the police."

Quickly checking the contents of the wallet, he found everything intact except the room key. Looking around, they found it near the doorway.

"He must have slipped it under the door after he went out, or dropped it on the way out."

"Check the luggage guys," Instructed Andy.

For the next hour, the family checked their luggage and went through all their belongings.

"Nothing's missing," said Cara. "Nothing's gone, and the wallet is back. What was he looking for, jewellery?" said Eric.

"Mum, where is the jewellery? Did you put it in the safe?"

"No, I did not. It's in the suitcase."

She quickly rummages through the suitcase, pulls out a black leather case. Opening it, she let a sigh of relief.

"It's all here."

"Now this is really strange," said Andy.

"Don't tell me the thief came all the way into the room, taking a huge risk just to leave my wallet back."

"Are we missing something. Maybe he knows we will go to the police and did not want any trouble as there was nothing much in the wallet and as you know the Credit Cards require a pin to make a purchase. One important point! The Hotel key card does not carry any information. So how did he know which Hotel and most importantly, which room?"

"He must have followed us from the Hotel, or has somebody on the inside working for him," added Cara.

"Worse, he could actually be working in the Hotel."

"You are right," said Andy.

"Any one of those options is a possibility. So now we can't complain as a wallet is back and nothing is missing. So we have to take the case back from the police."

"I don't want to stay in this Hotel," declared Cara.

"It's a huge risk and the thief might come back as he knows where we stay and God knows what he has done. What if he has installed a camera and is watching us right now."

"Not sure about that. I am not a millionaire nor do I work for the Government that he has to go through all this trouble."

"I am leaving, period!" announced Cara. "With two kids in a foreign city and a thief who has been into your hotel room, you must be insane to even question the idea."

"We've already paid in full for the room. We will lose everything. Why can't we request a different room?" argued Andy.

"No way! What if the thief is an insider and is still in the Hotel?Think about the kids. I don't care about the money. I just want to move to a different Hotel."

CHAPTER 11

Andy opened his laptop and started looking for a hotel booking portal. A few minutes later, he called out to Cara, "I've got a room! Look its close from here, just 10 minutes. If you are fine, I'll book the room."
Cara was desperate to leave the hotel and asked him to go ahead.

Andy called the hotel reception to request for an early checkout. The front desk manager offered to transfer the family to a superior room with no extra cost. Andy politely declined while he explained that his wife was not comfortable and it was not the hotel's fault, but just a personal choice.
"Can I view the CCTV footage of the floor? It might provide us with the pictures of the thief?"
"Unfortunately, we can only share it with the authorities. My apologies," said the Manager.
He went on to enquire about their choice of hotel. But Andy sternly refused to part with any information. Requesting for a taxi, he placed the phone down and set out to arrange their luggage.
Andy loaded the luggage into the taxi and asked the taxi driver to drop them at the Landmark Mall. Cara looks confused but stops herself from asking any questions. Heading into the mall, Andy heads over to the customer help desk and inquires about another exit.
"I don't want to leave any trace to the hotel where we will be staying. I felt this was the best way to avoid anyone from following us or enquiring with the taxi driver. Now we can catch another taxi and head over to our destination undetected."
Cara looked pleased with the efforts that Andy had taken to ensure their safety.

20 minutes later, they found themselves at the
Manraytan hotel. It was a small place with amazing
interiors and facilities. It was close to Victoria
Harbour but did not have the view the previous hotel
offered. The kids quickly settled in for the night and
Andy double checked all the windows and doors of
the room. The rooms were spacious and luxurious.
As Andy closed the curtains, he noticed a man staring
at the hotel. Feeling that he was acting paranoid,
Andy headed over to pick up a bottle of wine and two
glasses. Glancing once again through the window,
he noticed the same man standing a block away and
gazing at the hotel. "Cara", he called, but quickly
realised his blunder. The last thing he wanted was to
attract her attention, which would lead to further
complications. He was not prepared to usher the
entire family to another hotel in the middle of the
night and apart from that he had made sure that they
were not being followed. Cara looked at his worried
face and enquired if there was anything she should
know.
"Nothing to worry. I'm glad we switched hotels.
Now we can enjoy the rest of the holiday without any
further misadventures."
"True, but I still can't get the thought of someone
stealing your wallet and then going through all the
trouble to return it back by breaking into our hotel
room and not stealing the jewellery."
"Relax," he said handing over a glass of wine and
turning on the music. Holding her hand, they danced
to the music while Andy knew this was far from over.

CHAPTER 12

Andy woke up with startling thought. It was 4 A.M.
Walking over to the table, he gingerly switched on
the lamp making sure he did not disturb Cara. He
opened his wallet and started to comb through the
contents one by one. He opened the change pocket to
find his USB stick, which contained copies of his
passport, driving licence and Emirates ID (a personal
identification document for all UAE residents). It also
contained the passport copies of Cara and the kids.
Nothing had been deleted. Moving on, he removed
and checked on the credit cards, they were all there.
He then checked for his driving licence and Emirates
ID, both were in place. He emptied the cash and
counted, HK$ 1200 was also there. Just as he was
going to close the wallet, he realised the family photo
was missing. The photo was taken during their
wedding anniversary last year. Cara wanted to take a
photo before Eric's teeth fell out. It was a
monumental task to get Eric to do the photo shoot as
he insisted on not wearing a formal dress. It took a
great deal of cajoling and convincing that a pair of
shorts and T-shirt was not acceptable for a family
portrait. The photo would remain as a fond memory
for years to come. They made a large portrait, album
and 4 passport size copies for each of them to carry.
The official album of the photo shoot took one month
to be prepared as the photos had to be digitally
enhanced to look good. The result was amazing.
Even Andy was surprised at the quality of the photos
and recommended the studio to his friends and
family. So why would someone take only the family
photograph from his wallet? The only reason Andy
can think of was that the thief wanted to recognise the
members of the family. He was sure all his
identification documents were copied. This meant

that the person who stole his wallet knew his personal details, where he worked and how they looked. If this was a crime syndicate, then they could kidnap the children, Cara or even Andy and hold them for ransom. Having all the details and knowing how they looked could enable them to track their whereabouts in Hong Kong. His family's life was now in danger and his mind was racing. Should I cancel the vacation he thought and head back. If something should happen to his family, he must take the full responsibility and the guilt would probably kill him. He switched on his laptop and looked for the first flight out of Hong Kong. Unfortunately, all the flights were full and the flights via Kuala Lumpur would require a 9-hour layover. This meant they would have to spend an entire day in the airport before boarding the flight to Dubai. Since they were due to leave Hong Kong in three days Andy wondered whether it was worth the trouble or he's just being paranoid. His analysis of the situation was correct but was he overreacting about his fear of kidnapping and extortion. He needed advice and the best person he could think of was his dad. Ted Clarke was an engineer by profession and was known for his decision-making skills. He was one of the pioneers involved in hydropower generators. He had helped set up plants around the world. When Andy ran into a wall, he would reach out to Ted for advice and always looked up to his father's calm and collected approach to life. He had rarely seen him get agitated or overreact to situations. He called it as passive decision making and felt that most of the issues you have in a day will sort themselves out if you give them some time. Ted had done well for himself as an active player in the stock market and had gone on to make his fortune based on his wait and act philosophy. Ted was also consulted by friends and family for his decision-making skills but would only approach him when the time was not a constraint. It was 9 P.M., in London, Dad would be awake. It's time for his evening walk, thought Andy. He placed the call. The phone rang twice and Ted answered. Speaking in an excited voice, he said, "4 in the morning! It must be important, especially for a person who hardly wakes up before 7," he laughed.

CHAPTER 13

Andy quickly explained the situation to his dad and asked him what to do?

"You need to think about this situation carefully, as the thief returned the wallet and did not take anything except your family photo. So, the entire exercise was for the photo? To kidnap the kids or Cara doesn't seem to fit well, as he didn't have to come back to the hotel in the first place because he had the photograph with him already and your personal details too. I don't think the kids and Cara are in any danger. I think the person we are dealing with means no harm. But, I still can't figure out what he wants? Did you search the luggage and hotel room carefully? Has he taken something you are not aware."

"I have searched the suitcase dad. There's nothing missing, I am sure of it."

"How long do you think the thief had in your room from the time he picked your pocket?"

"Maximum 1 hour. I got off at the next station and immediately headed over to the police station after that I called the hotel." "So that's the only time he would have had but I guess he knew where you were staying because he was in your room before you called the hotel and the staff had a chance to change the keys. He timed the pickpocket in such a way that you could not get off the train."

"Yes, you are right! He picked my pocket as I was entering the train and there is absolutely no way that I could have got off. That gave him enough time to get away."

"The kids were already on the train, so I was in no position to run after him."

"Did you see him?"

"No, it was very crowded and I had no time to react. I did look around but there were so many people on the platform."

"There is something that we're missing. But don't worry too much. I don't think that you are in any danger. Keep the kids close and enjoy the rest of the holiday. If there is something then it will reveal itself soon. He has to make a move if he needs anything from you. Call me every day in the morning and evening so that I know you are fine. Let's keep this between us and I will not tell your mother. No point involving her, there's nothing much that she can do about the situation."

"Okay dad," said Andy.

In his eagerness to get his dad's input Andy totally forgot about Cara, who was now wide awake and was looking at him. Not knowing where to start he just said that it was dad.

"I heard everything," she said. "So what have you decided?"

"I just discussed the whole episode with dad. I think there is no real danger apart from that we have only two days. I have checked the airlines and the layover in Kuala Lumpur is between 9 to 12 hours. Being stuck with the kids in the airport for that long will be a real mess."

"I can't believe that you were going to keep all this away from me and put your family in danger, "said Cara.

"It's not like how it looks. I wanted to leave as soon as possible," said Andy, in his defence.

"Why don't you look at spending a day in Kuala Lumpur. We can see another city and relax without worrying."

"I have to look into the visa issue, plus the return tickets have to be cancelled. It's going to cost us, are you sure?"

"Yes, I am positive. Go ahead and do the booking. I'll make a call to the reception and ask them about the checkout and the cost associated with cancelling our existing booking."
"The flight to Kuala Lumpur leaves in six hours, " said Andy. "We need to get ready quickly and leave to the Airport."
"I have booked the Hotel tickets and requested for the documents required to apply for a visa on arrival. The Hotel sent us the letter with the reservation details which have to be presented at the visa desk at Kuala Lumpur for a Transit Visa."
The kids woke up disoriented, "What is happening?" they enquired.
"We're leaving for Kuala Lumpur," said Cara with a smile. "It's the capital city of Malaysia."
The kids were terribly upset about the change in plans as they wanted to visit Ocean Park in Hong Kong. Ocean Park comprises two main attraction areas: the Waterfront and the Summit, subdivided into eight attraction zones: Amazing Asian Animals, Aqua City, Whiskers Harbour, Marine World, Polar Adventure, Adventure Land, Thrill Mountain and the Rainforest.
The kids argued about why they needed to leave immediately. Slowly, the thoughts of being kidnapped took hold of them and they agreed to co-operate.

CHAPTER 14

The phone rang in the hotel room. Andy answered
and it was from the concierge desk. They had called
to inform him that the taxi has arrived and the
checkout papers were also ready. Ten minutes later,
the doorbell rang and the bellboy assisted them in
carrying the luggage down to the taxi. After settling
the bill, Andy got into the taxi and left for the airport.
Looking out of the window, he could not help but
feel sad. He had looked forward to this vacation, and
it is turning out to be a nightmare.
Andy was surprised as Eric pointed at the Pier and
started telling about how you could get there. The
kids had learnt the roads of the city so quickly.
Soon, Ava and Eric fell asleep in the back seat.
After 30 mins drive and crossing the bridge, they
reached the airport.
"We're here," informed Cara to the kids.

At the airport, the driver helped them with the
luggage as Andy dressed to get a trolley. Once inside,
they headed to the check-in counter. Loading the
luggage and obtaining the boarding pass, the Andy's
headed over to the immigration counter. Thirty
minutes later, they were sitting on the plane. As the
plane took off, Cara held Andy's hand, "Thank you,"
she said.
"I know it was a lot of trouble," she smiled and
looked out of the window. Then, Ava came with a
brown mail envelope with the strange symbol on the
backside. It was closed with a wax seal. "Who uses of
wax seal these days?" wondered Andy, taking the
envelope from Eva. "Where was it?" he asked.
"It was in my backpack, dad. It was open and it was
right on top."

Looking closely, he saw his name written on the envelope. Holding it up to the light, he could see a letter inside.

"Open it," said Cara.

Andy pulled out his phone and carefully placed the envelope on a tray. Taking photos of the seal on the back of the envelope and a close up of the seal he proceeded to open the envelope. Inside was a letter simply mentioning, "Sorry for the trouble," and US dollar 2000 in crisp new bills!!!

CHAPTER 15

"Oh, my God," shouted Eva. "That's a lot of money."
"Shush," whispered Cara.
"Keep your voice down."
Andy was lost for words.
"A thief who gives money! Now that's a first," he
said. "This episode is getting stranger and baffling by
the minute. Why would a thief give us money and
how did he put it in Ava's backpack?"
"When did you last check your bag Ava?" asked
Cara.
"Yesterday," she replied.
"When we checked out of the room, there was
nothing in there. This means it must have been put in
today, but by whom and when? The bag was with her
all the time and the only time they were removed was
at the immigration. It could have been the taxi driver.
But how did he know we were leaving, as the
message clearly states. This person or group were
very careful not to cause any harm to us and are in
fact making sure that we are compensated for all the
trouble they may have caused. But then, why?"

CHAPTER 16

"Two Italian and two oriental meals," said the hostess with a smile.
"Thank you," said, Andy.
The Italian meal was baked mac and cheese.
"Fruit and chocolate dessert. Anything else?" she enquired.
"Two glasses of red wine and two glasses of orange juice for the kids," requested Andy.

His mind quickly retreated back to the mystery.
"There's something that is missing here. The person or group, either targeted the wrong person and wanted to make amends, or they want something from us in the future, and this is a way of gaining our trust. Either way, we are out of Hong Kong, and I don't think they mean any harm. They have all my personal details and contact numbers. So it's not in our hands. Now let's hope for the best and enjoy the holiday."
"Hope it does not dampen the holiday, or what is left of it," murmured Cara.
The captain's voice cracked on speakers, "We will be in Kuala Lumpur shortly and the local time is 2:30 P.M., and the temperature is 38 degrees. Thank you for travelling with us and wish you a pleasant stay in Kuala Lumpur."

CHAPTER 17

Arriving outside the Kuala Lumpur airport, they were
greeted by the taxi driver assigned by the hotel for
airport pick up. He was holding a signage which had
'Andrew Clarke' written on it. Andy signalled him
and they all moved towards the car to load their
luggage.
Kuala Lumpur is the sixth most visited city in the
world, with 8.9 million tourists per year. Tourism
here is driven by the city's cultural diversity,
relatively low costs hotels, wide gastronomic and
shopping variety.

Arriving at the Hotel, the kids wanted to relax and
enjoy the hotel facilities. Andy was also tired and
agreed to spend the day by the poolside to enjoy the
sun and Jacuzzi. The next day Andy woke up to the
ring of his phone. It was his dad.
"Are you alright?" asked Ted.
"Why didn't you call?"
"Sorry, dad. I sent you an email."
He went on to explain what happened in detail.
Listening intently, Ted said, "Looks like the thief is
more scared of you than the other way around. Stay
in touch and call without fail."
Cara stretched and looked up questioningly at Andy.
"I had promised dad that, I would call him every day.
Just to make sure that somebody is aware."
"Ok, so what's the plan for the day? Let's hit the roads
of Kuala Lumpur. I have a lot of things to do here,"
said Cara excitedly.
"I will order breakfast in the room. That way, we can
get out quickly."
Andy drew the curtains and he could see the Petronas
Tower in the distance. Unlike the previous hotel in
Hong Kong, this Hotel was located right in the heart

of the business district to the northeast of the Old City Centre. The area was brimming with shopping malls, bars and five-star hotels.

Andy had booked a 24-hour bus tour and the pickup point was close to the Hotel. The double-decker, air con tourist bus made a circuit of the main tourist sites half-hourly throughout the day and was a handy way to get around. They stopped at KLCC, Jln Bukit Bintang, Menara KL, Chinatown, Merdeka Sq and the attractions of Tun Abdul Razak Heritage Park. There were many interesting places to see and enjoy. Shopping kept kids and Cara in a good mood. It was sweltering in the afternoon when the temperature touched 40 degrees. Lots of chilled water and ice cream helped in getting past the day.

Returning to the Hotel, the kids immediately jumped into bed. Andy was tired too, but, Cara looked fresh as a Daisy.

"Let's have some wine", she said, walking over to the bed. "I have a treat for you tonight!"

CHAPTER 18

"Good morning," said Andy kissing Cara on her cheek, who was slowly picking herself up and walking over to the window. Half an hour later, Andy had showered and dressed. He was wearing his favourite shorts and travel shirt. Stepping into the kids' room, he announced, "Get up sleepy heads," and switched on the lights and turned off the air conditioning.

"I hate it when you do that," screamed Eric.

"That's the best way to wake you guys up. Need to hurry up as we have made plans to take you to the top of the Petronas Tower. I've also got tickets to walk the bridge between the two Towers. It's going to be an amazing experience. So let's get going."

"Yay!!!" screamed Eric. "I will get ready in a jiffy".

"Now, don't forget to brush your teeth," joked Andy.

Andy went over to the phone to order breakfast and then sat on the sofa, switched on the TV to catch up on the latest news. Thirty minutes later, the family was waiting for the bus. The bus was on time and Andy wondered how they could maintain such accuracy given the traffic conditions. They headed straight for the open section on the first floor of the bus. It was their favourite place as it offered an amazing view of the roads and the surrounding. It's also a great place to shoot videos, as there are no obstructions, and you can also orient yourself about the roads. A short while later they got off at the Petronas station and walked over to the visitor's area. A long queue of visitors were waiting to enter the building.

The Petronas Towers, also known as the Petronas Twin Towers are twin skyscrapers in Kuala Lumpur, Malaysia. They were the tallest buildings in the world from 1998 to 2004 and remain the tallest twin towers in the world. The interiors of the towers highlight the Malaysian cultural inspiration to the design through traditional aspects such as fabric and carvings typical of the culture, specifically evident in the foyer of the entrance halls in the towers.

They admired the views from the Petronas Twin Towers Observation Deck and Skybridge. Then they set out to visit Bird Park which is a 60-hectare (150-acre) Lake Gardens, established in 1888. In addition to the 20.9-acre (8.5 ha) bird park, which was created in 1991, the gardens include an artificial lake, the National Monument, the Kuala Lumpur Butterfly Park, the Deer Park, Orchid and Hibiscus gardens, and the former Malaysia Parliament House. It is one of the world's largest covered bird parks.

CHAPTER 19

"No way. I am done," screamed Eric."I am not going anywhere today. You have been dragging me around and my leg hurts. Apart from that, you have not bought me any toy and have not had any good food, I want both!"
"Ok then. Let's go shopping and finish the day off with dinner to someplace nice," pacified Andy.
"Let's have Chinese," added Cara.
The family decided to visit Mid Valley Megamall and over dinner, Andy announced, "Tomorrow we leave to Dubai. Are you all happy to be heading back home?"
"Yes. We miss home," said the kids and Cara in unison.
"I can't wait to have a good long shower and sleep in my cosy bed," said Ava.
"I have to meet my friends and show them my toys," added Eric. "And most importantly, no more travel for another year."
"We will see about that," said Cara. "I have plans for your winter break."
"Here's to more fun and vacations," said Andy, raising a toast.

CHAPTER 20

"Dubai at last," breathed Cara.

The Andrew's lived in the Jumeirah, an upmarket neighbourhood dotted with cafes and shopping centres. It was close to Jumeirah Beach which was a famous and popular attraction for locals and tourists. Opening the apartment door Andy could feel the stale smell of the flat. Switching on the air conditioning, he found everyone walking away into their respective rooms leaving him to drag all the luggage.

"Thanks guys for your help!" he called out sarcastically and continued to pull all the luggage into the house.

He sat down on the sofa. It was back to the grind and how time passes so quickly when you're having a great time. He walked over to the TV and switched it on and got himself a cold orange juice from the refrigerator.

"I am going to have a hot bath and sleep for some time. Don't disturb me and please order lunch. I am not going anywhere near the kitchen for another day."

"No problem," shouted Andy. "We have another day of good food."

"Better watch your words, mister. Your adventure in bed will end if you continue on this path," she giggled.

Ducking down and grabbing his sword, the sombre figure swiftly plunged the sword into the enemy's belly. Making sure it cut through his organs.

"Dad," shouted Ava, shaking Andy to his senses. I must have dozed off, he thought, looking at Ava. "Mum asked you to order lunch and I want to have Arabic food. I really missed it."

Andy picked up the phone and called the restaurant
that provided great Arabic food and delivers at home
within minutes.

"You look preoccupied," enquired Cara over lunch.
"Just the same dream as in Hong Kong. It was one
step ahead on violence, not a subject over lunch. Post
lunch, Cara asked the kids to unpack the suitcases
and put the dirty clothes for laundry. Arrange the toys
so that Andy could put the suitcases into the store
room. Andy rolled over his suitcase to the bedroom
and started to unpack. As he was rolling it over to the
store room, Cara was also done unpacking and as she
closed her suitcase a clanking sound got both their
attention. Cara opened the suitcase again to look if
she had left something inside but there was nothing.
She closed the suitcase again there was a distinct
sound of metal against the lid of the suitcase.
"I guess it's broken," she said. "Let me have a look,"
said Andy. Opening the suitcase, he ran his hand
through the pockets. They were all empty. Feeling the
lining of the suitcase, he felt something at the bottom
of the lid. It felt like a tube as he held it with his
fingers and moved through the lining.
"It looks like an object inside the lining. Maybe
something broke during the trip and the pieces are
stuck inside the lining," said Andy.
And that's when he saw a small insertion in the lining
of the suitcase. It was about three centimetres long
and he could clearly make out that it was done using
a sharp object. He pushed it towards the opening and
could see that it was some sort of a cylinder but with
intricate designs on it. Andy pulled it out and handed
it to Cara.

"Looks expensive," she said. "Did you guys buy this and put it here or did Ava or Eric put it into the lining by mistake?"
"That's impossible," said Andy.
"There is no way that went in there by mistake, someone put it in there!"

CHAPTER 21

The cylinder was ten centimetres long and three centimetres in diameter. It was heavy and the metal looked like silver. It had intricate designs with lines and curves which looked confusing as they crossed each other. That's one piece of bad craftsmanship thought Andy. He shook it and there was something moving inside, tried to open the case but it was sealed. Cara spent the next few minutes examining the cylinder, but could not find an opening. Andy called both the kids and enquired if any one of them had bought or seen the artefact before. But both Eric and Ava did not have a clue. Eric examined the cylinder and started to rotate it in a clockwise direction. To Andy's amazement, the cylinder now formed a discrete design. He asked Cara to examine it closely. Then he rotated the cylinder. Cara could see it now. It's some sort of a symbol. Let's film it, using my phone. That way we can both examine it. Two minutes after filming, Cara stopped and Andy re-played the video. It was some sort of an octagonal design with minute symbols.
"The video is not very clear," said Andy. "Can you rotate it while I try to take a photo with my phone?" After a couple of tries, Andy gave up as the photos were no way close to capturing the image.
"This requires a professional camera to get the picture right."
For now, he had to manage with the video. After trying his hand at the cylinder a few more times, he gave up and left it on the table. In the evening, Andy returned to but did not find the cylinder. He went out to the kids' room and found Ava playing with it in front of the mirror. She was trying to look at the symbols. Finally, she said, "Dad, look at the design.

It changes when I turn it clockwise and when I turn it anticlockwise, it's a different one."
She was right. When you turn the cylinder clockwise the design only projects an octagon, but when you rotate anticlockwise it produces another symbol inside the Octagon. They were triangles that connected to form a star. When she rotated it faster, more stars appeared. Andy could now see three stars inside the Octagon made up of smaller triangles. That is one piece of work, he thought. Feeling foolish at his earlier assessment about the cylinder, he went over to Cara and explained what he saw. He rotated the cylinder as fast as he could, while Cara watched at it and said, "It looks familiar but can't place it."
"You have seen this design somewhere before?" he asked. "Maybe in Hong Kong, he asked?"
"No, I can't remember," she said.
"Dad!" startled, Cara almost jumped out of the bed.
"What is it, Ava?".
"I know where I have seen the symbol before. It was on the wax seal, behind the envelope with the $2,000!"

CHAPTER 22

"She is right!" said Cara, "It's the same symbol. Now it all makes sense."
"The money was given to take care of this cylinder."
"You mean, bring this object to Dubai? Why pay someone for it. We had no problem with customs and it was not detected by the X-ray machine at the airport." analysed Andy.
"It is metal, so is it something dangerous? It should have been detected or we just got lucky. What if there's a dangerous substance inside it? Do you know what kind of consequences it might lead to? We could have been in jail in Hong Kong for trying to smuggle a dangerous object. What if it's a Biohazard material inside that is designed to go off at a particular time?" blurted out Cara with bated breath.
"Now you're starting to scare me," said Andy.
"You're right. It is a possibility."
"I did shake the container a few times and the way we have been rotating it like a windmill, I can only hope whatever that is inside it, is not hazardous," said Cara.
"Throw it out of the house. I don't want it here," she instructed.

"Wait," said Andy, showing the money. "I am sure they will come to get it. If you don't have it, they can get very angry and to be honest, they are people who have been nice to us so far."
"Yeah, right!" yelled Cara.
"By stealing your wallet, breaking into our room and planting a potentially dangerous object in my suitcase."
"They gave us $2,000 maybe it's worth millions and not to mention potential imprisonment."
"Just keep it in the car."

"I thought of it," said Andy. But given the high temperatures and sweltering heat in Dubai during June, it does not seem to be a good idea. If the object inside is heat sensitive, it's going blow up and that would surely attract the attention of the authorities. That's the last thing we want. So, can we just keep it in the store room," said Andy.

"That's fine. Lock it and make sure the kids don't touch it," said Cara. Carefully handling the cylinder, Andy placed the cylinder in the storeroom and locked it. The potential danger to his family was starting to sink in. What the hell have I got myself into, he thought.

CHAPTER 23

The soldier stood with his sword and looks around.
He can hear the wailing of women and children at a
distance. Disgusted by the sound, he drops his
weapon and closes his ears with both hands. But the
noise gets louder and louder until it becomes
unbearable. He takes a short knife from his pocket
and plunges it into his ears!

Andy woke up sweating profusely. He could barely
understand and was completely disoriented. Walking
over to the living room he settles down on the sofa.
He switches on the TV and tries to get some sleep,
but in vain. Not knowing what to do, he switches on
the laptop and checked his work email.

He was not due in office until the start of next week.
Browsing through the email he found nothing urgent.
Closing his laptop and still unable to sleep, walked
around the house in the dark trying hard not to wake
the children or Cara. He will then have a lot of
explaining to do. Sitting in the balcony window, he
could see the cars moving in the early morning hours
when he caught sight of a soft light elimination
coming from the corner of the hall. Walking over, he
realised it came from the inside of the store room.
The door was open but he recollected locking it
earlier.

Oh no, he thought. Had the substance in any way
started a fire? He hurriedly went over to the kitchen
and using his phone screen light, picked up the fire
extinguisher. He slammed the door open expecting
fire inside. But there was no fire anywhere, just a soft
glowing light. Looking around, he found the glow
was coming from the cylinder. He gently touched it

carefully expecting it to be hot. But it was cold. Surprised Andy lifted it to find the whole cylinder illuminating.

It has been created by some kind of luminous substance. Never seen anything like this before, he thought. Could this be a toy, but the money and the symbol on the envelope indicated otherwise. The symbols had completely disappeared and instead, they were writings on the cylinder. Unable to believe his eyes, Andy stared at the script he had never seen before and wondered where did the symbols go?

There was a click on the storeroom door, someone was outside!

CHAPTER 24

Andy slowly called out, "Cara is it you?"

"Dad, it's me, Eric."

Looking sleepy and disoriented, "What are you doing here Dad?" he asked.

"I was just about to wake up Mama. I thought there was someone in the house."

"I was just looking for something," Andy said.

"In the store room?" enquired Eric. "At 3 A.M., It better be important. I am going to bed," Eric said and walked away.

"I am going to tell mama in the morning," threatened Eric as he went to his room.

"Don't you dare, you snitch!" warned Andy, but Eric was out of earshot.

The writings on the canister glowed in the dark and he had not seen anything like this before. He tried to take a photo but the light was too bright and the camera was unable to pick up the text. He finally wrote down on a paper and then went over to the laptop.

Switching it on, he started searching for the script on the web. There are about 6909 languages and 2197 dialects of various languages that are spoken in the world today. After a while, he realised that a language detection software was the only way out. He pulled out his smartphones and took a picture of the script and fed it into a translation software but only the popular languages were available.

CHAPTER 25

"What are you doing up so early?"
The question startled Andy as he was deep in thought. Turning around, he found Cara looking at him with a face filled with anxiety, and her eyes fell upon his hands holding the cylinder.

"What have you done? I thought we agreed on the part that you would leave that thing alone. Do you realise the recuperation of your actions? I am calling the police," she said.
"I can't take chances with my children. Let the authorities sort it out."

"You are overreacting", said Andy. Pulling her inside the storeroom, he shut the door. A few minutes passed and there was no reaction.
"What is it?" asked Cara. "I don't see anything happening". Slowly the cylinder started to glow.
"It is some kind of a chemical reaction," panicked Cara or,
"Is it some nuclear device?"

"Look!" Pointed Andy, as he started to turn it in the direction of Cara and she held her hands to her mouth in disbelief as the symbols turned into writings.
"How did this happen? Yesterday, it was just symbols that were inscribed on it."

Andy opened the door and let the outside light flash into the room. The writings disappeared and the symbols reappeared. "This is mind-blowing craftsmanship," said Cara.
"How did they manage to do this?"

"I think there is a coating behind the symbol which reacts to light and the writings appear. This is the only explanation I can think of," said Andy.
"I guess you are right," said Cara. "But what is the purpose of this device as it evidently holds something valuable and maybe the instructions on how to use it are on the cover. What script is it? I have never seen anything like this before."
"Yes. I searched on the internet but could not find anything like it, it's like looking for a needle in a haystack," added Andy.
"We have to open it and that is the only way we will know what is inside it."

"No way! It's too dangerous," said, Cara. "I can't allow that to happen. I don't want you to open it when I am not in the house. You promised me that you would not play around with that stuff last night and here you are holding it. I don't trust you to keep your word as your excitement will cloud your reasoning. I am going to lock this thing myself and I will keep the keys."
"Okay, so where are you going to keep it?" asked Andy slyly.
"That's a secret. It is only way I can make sure it remains safe."

CHAPTER 26

Damn it, thought Andy. Life was just starting to get exciting and he had not felt this way since his college days. His college life was very adventurous. Thanks to his crazy bunch of friends. Every week they would ride to remote locations on their customised motorbikes. They would compete to show off their bike's performance and design. They were also ardours of trekking and camping. They were real adrenaline junkies who would risk their life for some action. Andy attended rock climbing lessons during weekends and was always ready for any kind of adventure.

Once, while still in school, his classmate discovered an old abandoned British bungalow. They would spend time after school exploring this place and he fell through the rotting wooden floor to the basement. It was completely dark and he was terrified. There was zero visibility and he asked his friend to get help. He was struck in the basement for close to 30 minutes before help arrived. The caretaker lived in a small house nearby and had come prepared with a wooden ladder. The caretaker told them the place was not a bungalow but a court house where people were hanged. The hole through which he has just gone down was the morgue. The property belonged to a wealthy businessman from Manchester, who wanted to build an apartment Complex. They were waiting for the government to sanction the work. The place was haunted and was advised not to play around anymore. Even though the experience was nerve-racking, the only thing that kept Andy calm during those 30 minutes was the sense of adventure. He felt the same way now and had to get the canister from Cara.

Over the years, he had suppressed his love for mystery and adventure and inducted himself into family life. After Ava was born, he felt the need to concentrate more on his family. So, he kerbed his risk-taking behaviour to fulfil his responsibility as a father and husband. By the time Eric came along, Andy had been fully involved in the day-to-day running of the family, personal savings, work and family get-togethers had taken a priority. Andy had let himself loose during the few days of vacation and that was again a controlled environment where the safety of the kids took precedent.

Now after so many years, a sense of intrigue and mystery beckoned him. His mind, body and soul craved like parched earth that tasted the first drop of rain. He had to find a way to explore the secrets of the cylinder without endangering the family.

CHAPTER 27

When Andy finally woke up from sleep, he found
Ava sitting by his bedside.
"We are waiting for you to have lunch."
"What time is it?" asked Andy.
 "It's 1 P.M., dad." answered Ava.

Andy headed towards the toilet when he heard Eric
telling Cara, "Do you know dad was snooping around
the store room last night. I caught him with that
cylinder in his hand," he grinned and started to laugh
when he saw Andy standing behind him.
"Mama already knows you snitch. Ava, don't tell him
any secrets, he will probably tell everyone," said
Andy.
"Stop taunting my precious son. He is just doing the
right thing," said Cara.
Andy made an angry face at Eric and then laughed
out loud. After lunch, Andy switched on the TV and
grabbed some lemonade to drink.
"What are plans for the day? Thanks to you, we have
only half the day left" Cara whined.

"Don't worry. I will make every minute count. Let's
do grocery and catch up on a movie and dinner,"
offered Andy.
"I hate grocery shopping, dad. I'll pass," declared
Eric
"I am with him," said Ava. "Ok then, I will go later
and pick up the grocery. Let's do the movie and
dinner."

It was past 11 when the family returned home. The
kids went into their room and Andy heard a
commotion. "What happened?" he enquired heading
into the room. The cupboard was glowing.

Ah, so that's where she hid it, thought Andy.

"What is that dad?" asked Ava.

"Nothing to worry, Ava," comforted Andy. It was beaming through the clothes. Evidently, Cara never thought it would be so bright."

"It's just a light from my old phone," said Andy quietly concealing the artefact in a piece of cloth and headed out of the room. He placed it on the dining table and waited for Cara to return. 10 minutes later, he walked into the bedroom to find her fast asleep on the bed. It's my lucky day, thought Andy. He can now examine the artefact without any interruption.

CHAPTER 28

Just as Andy picked up the artefact, he heard Cara
walking out of the bedroom. There goes my chance,
thought Andy. As he had expected, she saw the
canister on the table and looked at him suspiciously.
"It was glowing in the hiding spot you chose. I was
under the impression you wanted to play it safe and
you choose kid's room of all places?" taunted Andy.
"I agree. You are right. I must find another place.
Until then let's put it in the store room. Promise me
you won't play around with it," said Cara frustrated
with the burden of safe keeping a strange object.
"Okay if it makes you feel better, I promise not to
touch this artefact."
There is no way I am going to get my hands on it, he
thought. Opening a suitcase, he placed the canister
inside it. He locked the storeroom and handed over
the key to Cara.
"I trust you, darling. You can keep it in the safe."
Next day, Andy was woken up by the sound of the
phone ringing. Hoping someone would answer and
put him out of this misery, he put his head under the
pillow. "Wake up! That was Jeena. She called to
invite us for her daughter's 2nd birthday party." Jenna
was Cara's assistant from work. She managed Cara's
appointments and helped her out with paperwork.
Over the years, they became good friends and usually
eat lunch together, also used to go out together on
pay day to celebrate. "I will not have the time to get a
gift once I am back at work. So let's do it today. Are
you fine with it?"
"It's fine with me. Ask the kids as they are the ones
busier than me."
Over breakfast, the family discussed what to gift the
two-year-old and it was finally decided on gold
jewellery and a toy.

The family set out to the Gold Souk in Dubai which is a traditional market (or souk). The souk is located in the heart of Dubai's commercial business district in Deira, in the locality of Al Dhagaya. The souk consists of over 300 retailers that trade almost exclusively in jewellery.

On arrival, they started exploring various retailers and finally entered a Greek shop called a Tenor Jewellers. They specialised in Greek origin designs and hand made traditional Greek artefacts. The storekeeper was a young man in his mid-twenties and was accompanied by an elderly gentleman. They looked related, but Andy was not sure. Cara spent some time looking at the collections and asked for jewellery suitable for a two-year-old girl. The shopkeeper immediately picked up some jewellery from the kid's section and Cara was impressed. "The jewellery designs are exclusive to our shop and we do not mass produce," said the elderly man. "The shop is owned by my family", the younger man added.
"This is my father and my grandfather who is not here today takes care of the Jewellery making. It is a family tradition and we have been in this business for generations. All the designs you are looking at is perceived by my grandfather. We incorporated new designs to keep up with the times, but the same old methods and craftsmanship have been passed on from generations to make sure that the same quality is maintained."

"Do you have a factory in Dubai?" asked Andy. "We have a workshop for repair and assembly, but we import it from Athens. We are very famous back home and our family has stores in all the main ports."

He proudly took out a brochure and gave it to Andy
which listed the store locations in Greece and in the
major cities of Europe.

"My entire family including six brothers and two
sisters are involved in the business and we have
started stores all over the world. We even got an offer
from a finance house to go public but my grandfather
declined as he wanted the business to remain with the
family."

"Have you found anything you like?" enquired Andy.
"Yes!" said Cara pointing to a chain with the Disney
character embossed in white gold.
"Excellent choice", said the younger man.
"I will take this," said Cara moving to the cash
counter.

"Why don't you pick up some fine jewellery from
our new collection for yourself, madam?" asked the
salesman trying to entice his customer. "We will give
you a good discount too."

"No, I came to get a gift. I will come back later," said
Cara.

As Andy was preparing to move towards the door,
his eyes fell upon a small cylinder crafted exquisitely
and placed on a stand. "What is that?" enquired
Andy.
"That is what we call a Taweez, as it is known in
these parts. You insert sacred scripts inside it and
hang it around the neck using a silver or gold chain.
We also have Taweez made for houses. It is the same
thing but bigger. It primarily holds a piece of paper or
secret substance which creates a positive energy. It is

also used to protect against the effects of the evil eye, envy and bad luck." explained the young chap.

 He continued, "We have been making these for generations. My grandfather is the one who designed this and will be in the store tomorrow. If you decide to buy, he can customise it with your name on it."
Andy jumped at the opportunity. What if the canister had something similar, he thought.
"I will drop by tomorrow," said Andy to Cara's surprise.

CHAPTER 29

The whole night, Andy kept thinking of Taweez. He
was curious to know if the artefact was indeed similar
to a Taweez. Would he be able to find a way to open
it safely or find a way of knowing its contents?
So the next day, he visited the store in the afternoon.
At the store, he was greeted by the younger guy
whom he met the previous day. After exchanging
pleasantries, he went into a small room inside the
store to fetch his grandfather.
"Hello," said the elderly man. "I am Julius. I believe
you are Andy. My grandson told me that you are
interested in the Taweez."
"Yes, that's me," said Andy trying to hide his
excitement.
"Please come with me," said Julius, leading Andy
into the inner chamber of the shop. The room was
brightly lit. In the middle of the room, was a table
with precision instruments. He offered a seat and
reached out for the catalogue. Opening it, Julius
showed the range of designs they could produce.
"I believe my grandson has told you about us. So I
will spare you the sales talk. Would you like to buy
or custom order? I make them myself. It took me
many years to perfect the skill." said Julius.
"What do they use it for?" enquired Andy.
Julius started to explain and share his profound
knowledge on this subject. "The evil eye is believed
to cause harm to a living or innanimate object. The
supernatural harm may come in the form of a minor
misfortune, disease, injury and in some case death.
 A person's fortune may turn sour overnight. They
may face sudden finnacial difficulties, have a acne
breakout before an important social gatering or may
find themselves in a bad mood for no reason. Objects
that are affected by the evil eye will break

unexpectedly, motor vehicles breakdown and electrical appliance will fail. It is said to originate from the eye of one who feels jealous or envious towards the victim or object. The best way to protect oneself is to wear a protective amulet. The Turkish Evil Eye pendant, which is made of blue glass, mimics the eye and is said to absorb the negative energy. In India, salt is used to remove Evil Eye and in Greece garlands made of garlic are hung in the house to wade off the negative energy." Feeling pleased with his explanation, Julius was now looking at Andy in anticipation.

CHAPTER 30

"So, is this supposed to help prevent bad luck?"
clarified Andy.

Julius was only happy to give more information.
"It depends on what you want? The power of the
Taweez comes from the script inside it. In the olden
days, the paper was not used but the bark of a tree
from the Himalayas. The material was durable and
would last for ages. The ink that was used was called
ashwagandha as it was made out of 8 ingredients. The
local priest would recommend a script depending on
the need of the person and we would be given
instructions on how to use it. Sometimes the scripts
had to be inscribed on the Taweez."

"You mean to say it's inscribed on the metal?" asked
Andy

"Yes, said Julius. It is a skill that is not easily learnt
and took me 25 years to master this art and my son
who is nearly 55 is yet to master it. He has been at it
for 30 years now and still cannot do it."

"Why not use laser?" asked Andy

"No, it does not work. The effect of the taweez is in
the script that is designed to interact with the outside
environment. It is created for two reasons. Firstly, to
stop negative energy from affecting you. Secondly, to
manifest your desires."
"The first taweez is typically designed with the script
locked into a cylinder and sealed so that it is
waterproof. The typical metals used for this one are
silver and brass as both metals have a high
electromagnetic capacity. When negative energy is

directed towards an individual, the Taweez encounters it first and traps the energy while the script dissolves it. I believe the paper inside basically neutralises the energy and that is why the case is sealed."

"The second type of Taweez are the ones that are rare to find as there are only very few artisans in the world who know how to make them. It primarily generates its own energy. My grandfather was one of the best-known artisans in the whole of Greece, who used to be called upon to make this Taweez for the rich and the famous. The Taweez used to take months of work to be prepared and the materials had to be selected with care. The chosen script had to be hand etched into the metal but the difficult part was to write on the metal so that the script was the same on both sides. This meant the script should be readable from the opposite side. Once ready, this was rolled into a cylinder through which air could pass and it was worn around the neck of the person who it was made for. The script contains the name of the person so if someone else wore, it will not work as it was created only for one master."

Andy's mind was racing. So, could the artefact be the second type of Taweez? Was it made for someone special or does it have the magical power to manifest the desires of the person who possess it, he thought.

CHAPTER 31

It was almost like Julius was reading Andy's mind when he said: "Taweez were created also to hold very important papers or documents, like a will of a king."

Andy was now totally tuned in and probed him further.

"The document canisters, were they made in the same way as a Taweez?".

"No. The ones for documents are much more complicated and difficult to make. The canister is designed for protection and is sealed from both ends. This prevents water and other natural elements from destroying the script. It can even be exposed to fire for a few minutes, but prolonged exposure would destroy the document. I have some documents my grandfather had shared on how to make these containers. Where did I put them?" muttered Julius to himself.

"In fact, I browsed through them a few weeks ago, while taking stock of the inventory, there it is!" he said reaching out to a book that was made of parchment paper with drawings and instructions on how to make the document container.

"Let me translate it for you," he said staring at the documents for a few minutes.

"Let's see, you first identify the material which has to be mixed with silver, brass and gold. The ratio is given here. This I believe is perfect for designing the case, as it allows to be very stable. The metal is made into a thin sheet and the outer layer is inscribed with the designs and has the royal seal of the house. Next, the sheet is rolled into a tube using heat and is then left to cool. A second sheet is then beaten to create another tube. This one has no engravings and serves as a second level of protection. The caps are sealed onto the inner metal tube with the documents inside. Since the document is flammable, they used the bark of a tree. Himalayan birch, is a birch tree native to the Himalayas, growing at elevations up to 4,500 m. There are specific uses of the different parts of the tree. The white, paper-like bark of the tree was used in ancient times for writing Sanskrit scriptures and texts. It is still used as paper for the writing of sacred mantras, with the bark placed in an amulet and worn for protection."

"The true brilliance of this system is in sealing the container securely so the documents can remain intact for centuries. This is done by applying a small layer of glue which seals the documents on the inside by allowing air to be removed creating a vacuum, preserving the paper perfectly for centuries. Now the only way to open the container is to break the seal which will release the vacuum. Once opened, you can't seal it back to its original state. This way, the owner of documents can know if its contents have been compromised."

CHAPTER 32

Andy was getting impatient. He wanted to find out if the artefact he is holding, contains any valuable document and if yes, how to open it safely. Also, what makes it glow? He wanted answers and quickly.

"Do you have any experience in making or opening these canisters?" He asked.

"No, my father was the last one trained in the art of opening one. The reason is that apart from storing documents, sometimes there is an acid kept inside as an insurance. It will break and destroy the paper, if not opened properly. It was also dangerous for the person opening the canister, as it could injure or burn them. Also, if the parchment was destroyed by mistake, then the owner would avenge him. Many artisans in my village have been killed over losing the documents. So, my father was the last in line to have learnt this art. By the time I was a teenager, people has stopped using these devices for storage."

Andy was contemplating if he must confess to the old man, that he was not here to buy a Taweez and let me in on the artefact. Andy was sure he was the right man to open the canister. But he wasn't sure if he should even open it. The artefact did not belong to him. The person who kept it had left no instructions. As of now, there was no real threat from the group or person. However, if something untoward happened to the artefact, they may harm him and his family.
It might be worth a fortune. What if the owner left it with him for safe keeping and land's up any day to retrieve it. He was sure they had his contact details. They must have made a copy of his ID, passport and other documents.

CHAPTER 33

Andy decided to give it a good thought before telling
Julius anything.
From all the pictures and samples, he had seen at the
shop he knew the canister was special. It was created
with great care and the illumination of the artefact
was a mystery.

He continued to probe Julius "Tell me, do these
things illuminate in the dark?" The old man was
startled, "I'm sorry, what did you just say?" he asked
with a surprised expression. Andy knew he should
not have asked the question the minute he said it. It
was too late, he had to just ride this one out and
handle it smoothly.
"I mean do these objects shine?" he asked changing
his words.
The old man suddenly relaxed. "Yes, depending on
the coating, we can give it a matte or glossy finish.
It's up to you."

Andy casually asked, "Why did you look so startled,
when I asked you if these things glow?"

"Oh that, well" hesitated the old man but he had
taken a liking to Andy and didn't want to disappoint
him. "I have heard my grandfather talk about a metal
that glows. He said it was from space. There was a
discussion at my house and I overheard him talk
about it. I believe the metal used to glow in the dark."
This is interesting, thought Andy. I could have never
imagined that it has been made with a substance from
space. "You mean to say it had a self-illuminating
property?"
"Yes, it does. Personally, I haven't seen it. Just as
you mentioned it now, I remembered this topic being

discussed at home many years ago, which caught all our fascination. "Have you come across anything like that?" asked the old man looking keenly at Andy. "Nope," said Andy with a smile and looked away casually.

CHAPTER 34

"So, what type of Taweez do you want? For protection, or purpose built?" asked Julius.
Andy felt trapped. He had to go with the flow if he didn't want the old man to suspect him.
 "I'll go for protection, where do you get the script from?"
Julius quickly bent down to retrieve a book full of scripts. "I had this done by a priest and it is very powerful. I have a script for almost anything under the sun."

Baffled at what he saw, he asked Julius. "So, you're telling me that these scripts have the power to bring specific results, but how? It's just a piece of paper with text on it. How do you guarantee results?"
"Good question," said Julius. "Have you heard of affirmations?"
"Yes. They are verses you say to manifest a specific result." replied Andy.
"Correct. Now how do they work?"
"I have no idea," said Andy. "I have never tried it out."
Julius, without being annoyed at Andy for asking numerous questions, patiently started to explain.
"The concept is that we are a drop in the ocean called life and each one of us have a path and destiny to fulfil. No matter how bad one's life maybe he or she has a role to play in the system of life. It's like a plant's life cycle. The plant starts life as a seed, which germinates and grows into a plant. The mature plant produces flowers, which are fertilised and produce seeds in a fruit or seedpod. The plant eventually dies, leaving seeds which germinate to produce new plants, said Julius. Every element has a role."

"The script is similar to this. The only difference is,
it's written down and kept inside a protective
container as the elements come in contact with one
another, It generates the energy which will aid in the
completion of the desired task.
In the case of protection, energy is trapped. And I am
not sure how it works but my guess is that the paper
neutralises the electrical impulse and acts like a
circuit breaker."

CHAPTER 35

It was all so new to Andy and it was too much
information to synthesise all at once. He looked at his
watch. An hour had passed. He had to get back home.
Andy quickly rose from his seat and thanked the old
man for his time and wisdom.
"It was nice meeting you. We will be in touch."

They shook hands and bid goodbye. Just as Andy
turned to leave, Julius called out for Andy and asked
him to come back. He quickly opened one of the
cupboards and retrieved a blue and white glass evil
eye pendant.
He attached the pendant to a black string and said
"This is for you. Wear this till I create the Taweez.
You should not wear multiple amulets as they will
interfere with each other and will not be effective."
Wondering what he was trying to imply, Andy
simply thanked him and left.

CHAPTER 36

The phone rings at Andy's residence. Ava answers it
and a deep voice on the other side asks for Andy.
"Dad, call for you," she said handing over the
receiver.
"Who is it?"
"No idea. Didn't give me a name."
"Hello, is this Andy?"
"Yes, how can I help you?" asked Andy.
The person on the other side spoke in a deep oriental
accent.
 "Hope you are doing well. Please allow me to
introduce myself. I am Tsang and I am calling you
from Hong Kong."
Andy's heart skipped a beat. Had they found him and
now what? he thought.
He gingerly asked, "What is this about?"
"You have come in the position of something of great
value and demand."
"What are you talking about?" queried Andy,
pretending to be ignorant.
"Please sir, let's not waste time. I know you have it
and all I wanted to tell you is that you were chosen to
have it."
"Have what?" persisted Andy.
Tsang ignored him and continued, "Please make sure
it does not fall into the wrong hands. Its power can be
misused to create havoc."
"We will get in touch with you when the time is right
to collect it."
"Collect what?" continued Andy, hoping for some
detailed information from Tsang.
"Good, I am glad you are keeping this up. It's the
right thing to do for your own safety. If you manage
to open it, do not reveal it to anyone. There are many,
who would kill to have it!"

Before Andy could react, the line went dead. He quietly placed the receiver back and tried the phone call history to get the last received number. It just said private number.

Can this be traced? I guess I must contact the local phone company and they will require a valid reason. Apart from that, I think they will need a court order he thought.

Cara questioned him from the next room, "So they know where we live and have our details."

"Well, that was expected. But again, they are not trying to harm us."

"How do you know it's a group?"

"Well, he said that I was chosen to have it. They will get in touch with me when the time is right. He told me that people would kill to have it and I must protect it and it should not let it fall into the wrong hands." informed Andy.

"So, what is it? A crazy psycho gave you some kind of a bio-weapon?" asked Cara, trying to figure out the object.

"One more thing, he mentioned that if I manage to open it, I should be careful not to reveal its content to anyone. Clearly, they do not have a problem with me opening the canister. But what's inside is something of a great value."

"If it was dangerous, he would have asked me not open it. On the contrary, I think he wants me to open it!" said Andy.

"Nonsense! You are just building this story to aid your curiosity. I know you went to the jewellers shop to find out more about this artefact and now you are steering this phone call to suit your plans."

Andy was startled at the words of Cara and the accusations being thrown at him but knew that it was the protective nature of his wife. She has been at her wit's end since the start of this mystery and the current situation was not helping.

"I assure you, it is not like what you think. I am telling you the truth. I know this whole episode is taking a bad turn. But I promise you, the safety of my family is my top priority."

Cara felt a pang of guilt for speaking out that way but held back on the apology. She thought its better Andy is cautioned, it will deter him from being reckless with the artefact.

CHAPTER 37

Alone, at last, I can finally try and figure out the gravity of the situation, thought Andy. Maybe I should call dad and appraise him of the latest development.

His father always advised him that when he found himself in a sticky situation, he should share it with a third person, who can give him a detached viewpoint. Andy decided it's best to discuss the matter with his dad. He also wanted to ensure that someone other than his family is up to date with the issue, should something untoward happen to them.

He placed the call to London. Ted answered it immediately.

"All okay?" asked Ted in haste, without the usual pleasantries.

"There's a new development. I received a call from the thief," informed Andy.

Bringing his dad up to speed on the call he waited for his inputs. "I will call you back in 10 minutes," said Ted and the line went dead.

Andy knew what Ted must be doing now. He would be writing down all the facts in a piece of paper, and drawing a connection chart linking all the events together and predicting the next step. Waiting in anticipation on his couch, he fell asleep.

Thirty minutes later, the phone rang and Andy surfaced from his deep slumber to answer it.

"Okay let's see," sounded Ted's confident voice through the phone.

"A person called Tsang called you. He is aware of the artefact and advised that it should not fall into the wrong hands. You are supposed to hold on to it, till they want it back. I don't think these guys are trying to harm you or your family."

Andy felt strange the way his addressed Cara, Ava and Eric as "your family" but he guessed. It was part of the process. Ted wanted to give a third person perspective and that was one of the reasons Andy reached out to him.

"Whatever you have in your possession carries great value and the people who spoke to you have asked you to keep it safe. The substance inside the canister is neither chemical nor biological in nature because I am sure Tsang would have asked you not to open it if that was the case. On the other hand, they have given you money and have warned about the perils involving the artefact. I am sure you have met them in Hong Kong. They have monitored your activities and have meticulously collected information about you before hiding the artefact in Cara's suitcase." reasoned Ted.

He continued "They are trying to protect the artefact from someone very powerful in Hong Kong. Why else would they take the risk of handing it over to a person from another country? The fact that Tsang cautioned you about divulging any information of the artefact or its contents with anyone implies that they are fine with you opening it. You were also informed they would come back for it at the right time which suggests that the substance is not time sensitive. Can you send me the photo of the artefact? Maybe I can think of a way to open it."

Andy informed Ted about his meeting with Julius, the Jeweller and the things he had learnt.

"Excellent!" said Ted. "Meet him and if you are confident you can ask him for his help in opening the artefact. I think it is vital that we know what is inside."

Both agreed on the next steps. Once this matter was out of the way, Ted enquired about Cara and kids. He also asked him about his work, while Andy enquired about his mum, who was taking a nap. They closed the call by agreeing to stay in touch and informing each other of any further developments.

CHAPTER 38

It was 4 P.M., Andy was waiting for a call from
Julius. Getting impatient, he decided to call him.
"Hello, my name is Andrew Clarke. May I speak
with Julius Please?"

"He just stepped out. I can give you his mobile
number if you wish," said a voice on the other side.
"Yes, please!" answered Andy.

Just as Andy dialled the number, Cara walked into
the room.
"All set?" she asked.
"For what?" replied Andy, with a puzzled look.
"Have you forgotten? Tomorrow is your first day of
work. It appears that you have enjoyed the holidays
so much that you don't remember you have to be at
work tomorrow."
 "Oh no, this has got me stumped. I have a lot of
things to do, where is my organiser?" Andy felt like
he was going in circles. His attention was completely
on the artefact and now the sudden realisation that he
had to get to work disoriented him. Not knowing
where to start he pulled out his organiser and quickly
jotted down the things he needed to do before work.
The list was long. He usually divided the tasks over a
couple of days. That way he could enjoy his holidays
and not feel the strain. Andy was disorganised by
nature but he was forced to get organised as it was
the difference between failure and success. Andy was
not gifted with a great memory and that always lead
to embarrassing situations. To tackle this problem, he
started using a notebook to jot down the names of
places and people he visited. Andy had a daily log of
tasks. He integrated this list into his schedule so
nothing slipped through the cracks. He quickly

created a task list and took an inventory of the activities that needed to get done. The meeting with Julius had to wait till he got through the first week of work.

CHAPTER 39

5:30 A.M., the alarm rings by Andy's bedside.
Turning it off, he walks over to the bathroom quickly
washes his face and changes into his track pants and
T- Shirt. 20 minutes later, he starts running on to the
Jumeirah Beach Cornish.

Andy never worked out during weekends and on
holidays. But on work days, he made sure he got out
every morning and ran for 45 minutes around the
Cornish. It kept him active and sharp at work. Soon
after he reached home, he walked over to the
breakfast table with the newspaper in his hand. Andy
was religious about having at least two meals which
are mostly breakfast and dinner with his family. He
believed it kept the family together and Cara felt the
same way. It allowed them to take stock of day ahead
and the day that went by. After school activities,
other events were shared during breakfast.

Andrews had employed a domestic help, Jane, from
the Philippines. She was on annual vacation and was
not expected back until next week. They usually
coordinated the travel plans of the family with Jane,
but this time around, she had extended her vacation.

Andy's office was based in the business district, a
hub for the technology companies in Dubai. The
morning traffic was horrific and getting a parking
spot outside the office was a challenge. One had to go
around constantly finding a parking spot.

Andy arrived at work and walked over to the
reception desk. He was greeted with a big smile from
Lizzy, the super-efficient, multi-talented receptionist.

He spent the next 10 minutes talking about his trip
and then he placed a souvenir which was bought from
Hong Kong Disney Land in a glass cabinet, a custom
that was followed by employees who returned from
their vacation. The cabinet was overflowing with
souvenirs from all over the world. The other custom
was to get chocolates and confectioneries. Opening a
box of Chinese Fortune cookies, Andy placed them
on the receptionist desk for others to help themselves.

Andy walked over to his desk and found some
envelopes. It was mailed from his P.O. Box. Going
through the mails, he found the bills that he had
expected and then stopped. There was a plain
envelope with the Hong Kong stamp. Andy quickly
glanced around to see if someone was watching him.
Then quickly, he took out his phone and
photographed the front of the envelope. Andy could
tell by looking at the text that it was printed using a
dot matrix printer. These printers were used by shops
for printing receipts but were rarely used in homes
and offices. Turning around, he stared at the same
seal. There was a letter clearly folded. Opening it he
found the sentence, "We Know, You Know."

CHAPTER 40

Andy quickly tucked the envelope into the suit pocket and rushed out of his office to his car, as he did not want anyone noticing the letter. Once in the car, he pulled out the letter from his pocket to study it more peacefully. He looked at the stamp. It was sent on the day they left Hong Kong. Clearly, this was not a threat. It was sent to let him know that they were aware that he had the artefact. They also wanted him to realise, that they knew where he worked.
 Andy flashed the paper against the light. There was nothing but a watermark of the seal. Andy pondered if the group took pains to create watermarked stationery. They must be keen to brand their communication or could this be a corporate letterhead? Was this just the logo of a company and not of any secret group?
Should I tell Cara? He contemplated. She could overreact and things would only get worse. Picking up his phone, Andy called Ted and quickly explained about the contents of the letter. Ted said he will call back in ten minutes. Andy cut the phone and waited. Twenty minutes later, he got impatient and rang Ted. He picked up immediately and apologised, "Sorry, I was online looking for that Logo you sent me earlier. I cannot find the logo on the internet but I recognise the collection of triangles that make the flower. The triangles form a three-dimensional image but because of the boxes, it's not clearly visible. Have you heard of Sri Chakra?"
 "No, never heard of it." replied Andy.

CHAPTER 41

"Sri Chakra is a design that is formed by nine interlocking triangles that surround and radiate out from the central point. The two-dimensional Sri Chakra, when it is projected into three dimensions, is called a Maha Meru. Mount Meru derives its name from this Meru like shape. These nine triangles are of various sizes and intersect with one another. In the middle is the power centre, visualising the highest, the invisible, elusive centre from which the entire cosmos expands. The triangles are enclosed by two rows representing the lotus of creation and reproductive force. The broken lines of the outer frame denote the four openings to the regions of the universe." explained Ted.

He continued, "But what I can't fathom is the use of Pentagon as a top layer of the outer circle. This is a mix of a Pentagon and Hindu symbols. Whoever crafted this, is a genius."

"Why do you say that?" asked Andy.

 "Well, Sri Chakra channels energy from four directions-North West, East, and South. But the Pentagon channels energy from eight directions, North, South, East, West and the secondary directions; North West, South West, South East and North East. They have super-imposed the secondary directions on to the primary. It's such a simple way to improve the existing system. Whoever did this, has a lot of knowledge of the occult. To combine the two symbols of different cultures and yet enhance the existing system requires prior training. The Sri Chakra can only be created by trained artisans and the art is passed on through generations. There are no books on how to create one." informed Ted.

Andy listened intently as Ted continued to share his knowledge of the topic.

 "The design has to be precise. Any deviations of the triangles will render the drawing ineffective. To create a seal for the letterhead they must have the real object with them."

Andy was getting impatient and just wanted to know the next step. He interrupted his dad "What should I do now?". Although he was 32 years old, he sounded like a child before his father."

"Just don't do anything. These people are making the move, so let them do it. Do not open the artefact, just in case they come looking for it. Keep the channel of communication open." Advised Ted.

CHAPTER 42

Walking back into the office, Andy bumps into Omar.
"Hello! Welcome back," he exclaimed with a big smile.

Omar, despite being the owner of the company, preferred to be addressed by his first name and did not maintain power distance.

"How are you doing?" enquired Andy. He picked up a box of Fortune Cookies and a metal statue of Buddha from his desk. He handed over to Omar. "Something for you from Hong Kong."

"Thanks. Come into my office and tell me about your vacation."
30 minutes later, Omar was still talking about his adventures in Hong Kong.
He was well travelled and had been to most of the famous tourist destinations around the world. It was his dream to retire and pursue his wanderlust and meet new people and experience various cultures.
The phone rang at Omar's desk. Andy used this opportunity to excuse himself.
As Andy stood up to leave, Omar instructed to meet him later in the day, along with Tony.

Stepping out of Omar's office, Andy was pushed and tripped. Bracing himself against the wall, he saw Mary, his co-worker giggling.

Mary was a 23-year-old management graduate and this was her first full-time job. She was a quick learner and had a perfect balance of motivation and reliability. She was keen to climb up the corporate ladder but was also willing to wait for her time to come. She has graduated from a top university in Wales and interned for a couple of months in London before she was lured by her friend who was living it up in Dubai. The sun, sand and beaches were too difficult to resist for someone of her age. Soon she packed her bags and landed in Dubai. But with no prior experience, she was struggling to find work.

At a time, when she was almost ready to give up and return to London, she received a call for an interview with Andy. During the selection process, Andy noticed that she was very sharp, highly motived and self-driven. He hired her right away and asked her to start the next day. She felt greatly indebted to him for having given her the opportunity and believing in her.

During onboarding, Andy was open about his memory problem. From that moment on, she made sure that Andy never forgot anything. Mary would call him before important meetings and SMS the day before. It was not part of her job but, she did it as a friend.

"Lucky, I didn't have coffee in my hand," quipped Andy.
"How was your trip?" asked Mary.
"What happened?" she demanded. "No calls or messages? I know you were on vacation but weren't you supposed to be back in town last week?"

 "Sorry, I was busy with some domestic stuff," replied Andy.
 "I don't believe a word. You're up to something and I'll find out soon." chided Mary.

Andy casually enquired her about his mails, calls and posts to check if she knew about the artefact. He breathed easy, as he noticed nothing was amiss.

Just then, he felt a tap on his shoulder. It was Antony Williams, Tony to his friends and colleagues. He is a 56-year-old chubby and jovial guy. For the past 6 months, he has been trying to lose his belly fat but was equally working on the beer. He was advised to take up yoga but found it hard getting into the various poses. He then hit the gym with a personal trainer. After three months, the trainer quit saying, "If you are going to sneak out for a burger and beer every day, I can't help you."

 "Hello Andy, how are you doing? No emails or calls. Look like you had a good holiday?" Jibed Tony. After Andy ran through his trip details and informed him that Omar wanted to meet them in his office.

"Oh, it must be about the event in London next week," said Anthony.
"Next week!" shouted Andy in disbelief.
"It's the Annual Technology week in London, and we are participating in the Expo and conference. Don't fret my friend. A media company is taking care of the preparations. So, pack your bags as we are both flying to London next week!" enlightened Tony.

CHAPTER 43

"What a day?" Andy thought while driving back home. As he was parking, he spotted Cara driving into the garage.
"Where have you been? I took the kids to the supermarket to get the grocery for the week. Looks like you had a busy day. I didn't get a call from you the whole day, what's up?"

"It was hectic. I had lots to catch up," said Andy. "I have to go to London next week for an Expo."

"Oh, I love London. Can I come too?" interrupted Eric.

"Sorry pal, it's an official trip. Apart from that, your school starts in one week," replied Andy.

"Take us along, dad. We will stay at grans and won't bother you." pleaded Ava.

"Tickets are expensive at this time of year. Secondly, you guys just got back from a holiday, and I will be gone all day. So it's not worth it." said Andy trying to make sense to the kids.

"Whatever!" said Eric walking towards the lift.
Cara smiled, "How did it go? Looks like they were waiting for you."
"Yes. It was a surprise. We did not have any plans of participating till last month. But now, suddenly they decided to enrol in both Expo and Conference. Anyways, it's a chance for me to meet up with my mum, dad and of course my cousins. It's been long." said Andy, as he picked up the grocery bags and walked towards the lift.

"So, it's going to be a bachelor party in London, is it?" taunted Cara.

"Come on we're just the bunch of responsible and well-behaved adults." Andy teased.

Cara knew better. Andy's cousins were responsible men, as far as they were on their own. But when together, they were a wild bunch feeding off each other's energy. The last time she visited London, Andy and his cousins walked over to the neighbourhood bar and returned after two days. She received a message on her phone at 1 A.M., stating that there are off to visit the Stonehenge in Scotland. The next incident was even stranger. As a newly married couple, they went to visit his cousin Timothy in the Midlands. After travelling for nearly 2 hours by train, they got off at a small village much before their destination. Timothy was waiting outside the train station with the minivan he had rented for the day. They set off to a local restaurant where the beer was supposed to be excellent. They had got off the train just for a glass of a beer! Cara was livid and didn't speak a word till she reached Timothy's house. Cara always wondered what dark secrets they shared with each other. But she stayed clear of wanting to know hearing stories of their ex-girlfriends and crazy party life that may upset her. Jerry and Ryan had enjoyed their bachelor status and were in no hurry to get hitched. However, Jerry had recently announced that he will be tying the knot next year. He was dating Debbie for the past few months and everyone in the family was surprised and happy that he has finally decided to get married. The wedding was to be held in London and the family had already started preparing for it.

CHAPTER 44

Andy got himself a cup of coffee and went into his study. His mind was pre-occupied about his trip to London. He had almost forgotten about the artefact. His cell phone rang by his desk. He answered it.

"Good evening", said an excited voice. "It's Julius from Tenor Jewellers."
"Good evening Julius, hope you are well?" answered Andy.
"I will be inserting the script on Saturday. So, you can pick up the Taweez anytime on Sunday," informed Julius.
"Why Saturday?" asked Andy.

"Well, it is based on the planetary movements. Every script has a particular day and time of inception. The energy present during the time helps the script," replied Julius.

"Thank you, I will collect it on Sunday," said Andy and hung up. Andy had a busy week ahead of him. He had to arrange for his passport to be renewed, meet clients, pay the school fees for the next term, renew his domestic help's visa, the list was endless.
"Dad!" Ava's voice interrupted his train of thought. "You have a call."
Andy was so pre-occupied with the task at hand that he had not heard the phone ring.
"I think it's the same man who called you from Hong Kong," whispered Ava.
Before answering the phone, he looked at the log. It said "private." They must be using a calling card or a computer with the VPN he thought.
"Hello, Andrew. It's Tsang, how are you?" he asked politely.

"I am doing well," replied Andy.

"Hope you received the letter?"

"What is the meaning of all this?" enquired Andy.

"Everything will be revealed soon. There is danger all around and you must be careful," warned Tsang.

Andy wanted to ask Tsang about the contents of the canister. Before he could ask, Tsang said, "I will be in touch. Use a UV light pen on the letter you received."

The phone went dead before he could react.

CHAPTER 45

Andy took out the letter and placed it on the table.
There was nothing on the page except the words-"We know, you know".
He switched on his computer and googled-"UV Light Pen". These were used by security companies to mark objects. When written using these pens, the writings are not visible to the naked eye. But when exposed to the UV light they seem to appear. Now that's a nice way to send the secret message, thought Andy.
But where do I get a UV light pen?

He got out of the house before anyone noticed and drove down to the local store. Scanning through the stationary section, he found a yellow pen with the UV light on top. Excited, he returned home. Cara spotted him heading towards the bedroom "Where were you? I called you on your mobile, but you had left your phone at the desk." Before Andy could answer, Ava jumped in "Dad was it the same guy who called you last time from Hong Kong."
Cara's face turned red with anger.
"Thanks for that Ava. Your timing is perfect."
"What did he say?" she continued ignoring Andy's comments.

Andy was contemplating if he should share more information with the kids.
They cannot be trusted to keep this a secret. Their school opens in a weeks and Eric was sure to discuss it with his friends. He had a weeks to make them forget the whole episode.
"I just went to fill petrol," said Andy trying to deviate from the topic.
"What did the guy on the phone want?" asked Cara.

Andy pulling Cara over to the bedroom told her what
had transpired and pulled the letter from his pocket.
She was visibly shaken.
"When were you planning to tell me this?"
"Look. I understand the whole episode is exciting,
but you have a family to take care. I will throw that
object out. I don't care what happens."

Andy was not listening. He was shining the UV light
on the letter but nothing appeared. He tried it again,
but there were no signs of a message. Maybe I am
missing something. He slowly ran the beam of light
through the entire paper with no luck. He repeated the
same on the other side of the paper.
"What am I missing?" he uttered in frustration.
"I guess you got the wrong light," added Cara.
"No this is it. I researched," confirmed Andy.
"What did he tell you exactly?" asked Cara.
"Tsang asked me to use the UV light on the letter.
Wait a second. Andy bolted to the bathroom and was
about to dip the letter in water when Cara asked him
to stop.
"What are you doing? Let's take a copy of the letter
first. Just in case, you destroy it."
Cara carefully took a photo of the letter and then
made a copy. Andy opened the tap and soaked the
letter in water. He went to study table and beamed the
UV light on it. At the first there was nothing but then
a drawing started to appear Cara stepped back and
quivered as the picture started to unfold.
"It's a map!" she yelled.

CHAPTER 46

"Unbelievable!" murmured Cara.

"Evidently, there is an acid layer on the paper. When the water falls on it, the picture becomes visible under the UV light and once it dries the picture disappears. They have gone to a large extent to hide this map. Let me take a photo." said Cara.

"It's a map alright. But, I can't recognise any of the writings on the map. I think it's the same language on the artefact," added Andy looking keenly at the map.

"You are right," said Cara looking at the writing on the map.

"Get the artefact, and we can verify it." said Andy. Cara went over to the store room and bought the canister.

"That's weird," she quipped. "It wasn't glowing when I found it but now, I can see it lighting up."

"Maybe it works with touch or friction or just movement," Andy offered his analysis.

"Like glow sticks that glow in the dark when you shake them?" clarified Cara.

"Yes, but Julius had told me that he had heard of a metal that glows and I believe it came from space." Cara looked at him in amazement. "Just what else have you discussed with him?"

"General stuff. Nothing specific about the artefact. The old man likes to share his knowledge," replied Andy.

Looking at the alphabets, they could see the similarity between the two.

"Ok, it's the same script, but how to find out its name? Do you know any language expert?" asked Cara.

"We have hit a roadblock again. I hope this is not a place we have to go. That will be crazy. I can't figure

out the country but I can tell you this is not a general reference map. It's a topography map. Look at the mountainous regions, the curve here looks like a river and I guess this cut is some kind of a pass," explained Andy.
"So, what exactly are we looking for in this map?" asked Cara.
"There is no way we can find this place. Because, it is specific to an area. Not a state or country. This whole area may be spread over 100 or 200 kilometres maximum and to find a place like this is impossible from a satellite.

Andy compared the script on the map with that of the artefact and uttered, "The person who copied this map does not know the language either. Look at the blots of ink in some of these letters. It's like the person who copied, stalled in the middle of every letter and then continued."

"Why would someone send us a map of a place and in a language that they themselves don't understand, and what's more puzzling is that they are expecting us to figure it out?" queried Cara.

"Could it be a clue to what lies inside the artefact? If it has a map, then it makes sense why people could kill for it. Especially, if it leads to a treasure." said Andy.

"Let's start by searching for all languages spoken in and around Hong Kong, past and present. Since we got the artefact from there, we might also find the topography in the region," suggested Cara.

"Okay. Sounds like a plan. So, you are interested in
knowing what's inside the artefact after all?" smiled
Andy.
"Of course, if it's a treasure. This could be one of the
last hidden treasures one could ever find in this
world. Hopefully, no one has found this one," replied
Cara enthusiastically.

CHAPTER 47

They spent next few hours looking for a script that matches the one on the canister. They had scrutinised through most of the scripts that are either active or extinct. They were not even able to get a close match. It was a dead end and they concluded that it must an ancient script.

"Let's call it a day," said Cara stretching. "I have an early day tomorrow and you have work."

Andy reluctantly closed the laptop and went to bed. The next day, Andy found himself catching up on emails from the past week and scheduling appointments with clients. He had to coordinate with his counterparts in other countries and arrange the plans for the conference. During lunch, he called Ted to update him on the events.

"A map you say. Send me the picture," said Ted. Andy hung up and sent him a snapshot. Twenty minutes later, Ted called back.

"This is an amazing piece of work and a good reproduction of the original. The language is the key. Tsang somehow expects you to either know or learn the language. I don't think this is the entire map. It's only a part of it."

"Why do you say that?" asked Andy.

"You see, there are no specific places mentioned. It's more like a terrain map. I don't think this map was important, or he would not have put it in the mail. He's surely holding back the rest. However, it might be a clue as to what's inside the artefact."

"I agree," said Andy. "But he could have just sent me any map. Why send one in a language I can't read."

"That's a mystery. Why don't you ask him? Tell him to stop these games and let you know his intentions. Threaten to do away with the artefact, If he does not come clean with you. He owes you that much. You

have a family to take care of and you cannot be
expected to expose yourself to danger," advised Ted.
Andy agreed and hung up. But the only problem was
he could not reach Tsang. It was one-way
communication. He had to wait for his call to end this
suspense.
In the meantime, Andy put a plan of action to keep
himself busy and not to indulge in this pursuit. He did
not want to do anything he would regret.

CHAPTER 48

It was 6 P.M., when Andy rang the doorbell. Cara opened the door with a smile.
"How was your day? You never called."
Andy realised he had been so preoccupied the whole day that he had ignored his family. Andy had not spent any time with the kids over the past few days, thinking of the artefact.

"Check if kids want to dine out, Italian maybe?" suggested Andy.
By the time Cara turned around to check with them, "Yes!" screamed Eric.
"I will change in 5 minutes."
"Let's leave by seven. I am hungry," said Ava, who now joined the conversation.

"Are we celebrating something?" checked Cara.
"Nah, we have not been doing things together since we came back from our vacation. I have been preoccupied with the artefact and just wanted to spend some quality time with you guys. I will be off to London next week. So, I want to make the most before I leave."
Cara moved towards the bedroom to get dressed for dinner. Meanwhile, Andy looked around for the artefact. But it was not in the living room. As he entered the bedroom, he saw Cara pulling a dress from the closet. He looked around and found it on the study table. As he got closer, it started to glow.
"That's strange," said Cara. "I tried my best to make it glow today."
"Maybe it's was the daylight from the window interfering. Now that it's dark, you are able to see it." inferred Andy.

Cara disagreed. "It was completely dark. I ensured
that the blinds were drawn. Trust me, it wasn't
glowing."
"Never mind. I'll get some coffee, and check on the
kids," dismissed Andy.
Two minutes later, Cara called out for Andy. He
walked over to the bedroom and saw her staring at
the artefact.
"What is it?" he asked.
 "It only glows when you are near it." uttered Cara.
"What do you mean?"
"The artefact only glows when you come near it. Just
step out of the room, and let's see if I'm right."
Andy moved away from the room, and it was still
glowing.
"It's just your imagination running wild."
"Close the door," said Cara. "Come in," she shouted.
"I was right. It stopped glowing when you closed the
door and look, it's glowing now. I'll record it on the
phone so you can see for yourself."
Andy exited the room and closed the door behind
him. A few minutes later, he returned to find the
artefact glowing mildly. Cara was waving her phone
at him. He replayed the video to find she was right.
He repeated the exercise to find was it consistent with
Cara's findings.
"Could it be my clothes?" he wondered.
Let me change. It could be the keys or something in
my pockets that may be activating it."
Andy rushed to the bathroom and emptied his
pockets, threw in his clothes into the washer and
stark naked, he walked into the bedroom. The
canister began to glow softly.
Cara was surprised to find Andy naked.
"It stopped glowing the minute you stepped out!"
grinned Cara.

"Are you trying to use this to get into bed?" she winked.
"Why not, can't get undressed for nothing," teased Andy.
But this new development bugged him.

CHAPTER 49

"This is getting crazier by the minute," said Cara.
"Let's try if it glows when kids are around."
Andy quickly dressed and rushed the kids into his
bedroom and stayed out. 10 minutes had passed
since the kids entered the room, and he was getting
curious.
Andy asked, "So, is it glowing?"
"Nope, you can come in now," replied Cara.
 Cara was sitting on the bed holding the object which
was glowing brightly.
"How can it possibly glow when I'm around?"
enquired Andy.
"It is able to see you, remember the first time you
saw the glow from the store room."replied Cara.
"What nonsense!" exclaimed Andy? "You mean to
say it has vision?"
 "No. What I am suggesting is that it might have
some kind of technology that enables it to detect you,
like Bluetooth and NFC."
"Ok, let's assume it uses a technology similar to NFC
or Bluetooth. But then, the parent and child have to
be on the same software or gateway, right? Where is
the connection? Let's check out your theory by
placing it inside the closet and see if it glows."
Two minutes later, Andy walked into the room. Not
saying a word, he slowly peeped into the shelf. Cara
had wrapped the object in a cloth and kept inside.
There was no glow. Andy then instructed her to
remove the cloth cover and place it back. He entered
the room and there was no glow. Andy peeped into
the storage compartment through the cracks and the
object started to glow.
"This is no Bluetooth technology, but more on the
lines of NFC. It can see me and works only on visual

contact. But how can an inanimate object see or recognise me?"

CHAPTER 50

"My head is reeling," said Cara. "This is all a little too much for me."
"Mine too," said Andy. "How do we figure out what this is? Oh no, I totally forgot to send out an important mail. I will be right back."
When he returned from his study, Cara was deep in thought.

"I have been thinking. This artefact was given to you because you were the chosen one," continued Cara.
"How did they know, you are one? Maybe they saw this object glow when you were near and decided to give it you."
"Firstly, said Andy. We moved around a lot during our vacation. It would be safe to say that Tsang was not taking it around with him for the artefact to glow in public."
"Secondly, even if the artefact glowed when I was around, how did Tsang specifically know that he had to give it to me?"

"Do you mean to say even Tsang doesn't know what it is, and is only following orders. That's impossible," said Cara.
"Yes. I don't think they know what's inside it," replied Andy.
"Why would they give away something of great value to a stranger?" challenged Cara.
"You do have a point. I think we should concentrate on the artefact and the language it projects. That is the key," suggested Andy.
"But I have spent a lot of time online trying to find a match," sighed Cara.
"We need to find a linguist or a historian."

"Bingo!" said Andy. "Nick's dad in London is a professor of history at the local university. I can run this past him, for his advice."

"Good idea," said Cara. "But I hope you are not planning to take the artefact with you to London. If it gets detected at the Airport, you could land yourself behind bars, and there's no way I can help you."

"I will just take photos and videos of the artefact," pacified Andy.

This is just trouble, she thought. Andy and his cousins, with such dangerous information, could run wild with it.

CHAPTER 51

Cara was busy on her first day back to work, when her phone rang. When she quickly glanced to find two missed calls from Andy. Must be important, she thought, "Hello, honey! I was in a meeting. What's up?" answered Cara.

"The passport renewal application was accepted and I should get it within 48 hours. I have to do some shopping in Bur Dubai for the folks back in London. So, when are you free?"

"Let's do it this evening, as I have a busy day tomorrow. Four meetings have been lined up with board and investors," informed Cara.

"Okay, see you in the evening. Why don't we take kids with us and dine out?" offered Andy.

"Sounds great." said Cara.

Bur Dubai is a historic district in Dubai. Its home to several mosques including the Grand Mosque with the city's tallest minaret, and the blue tiled Iranian Mosque. The country's only Hindu temple is situated between the Grand Mosque and the Creek.

It is home to several popular places for tourists including renovated historic buildings and museums. The district has many shopping streets and souqs (or souk), including the textile souq near the Abra boat station.

They shopped for some authentic Arabian Sweets, dates and souvenirs.

"Ok guys. My shopping is done. Where would you all like to dine?" asked Andy.

"Pizza!" was answered in unison. They went to a pizza place known for its wood-fire oven pizzas and the kids loved it.

The next morning, Andy was just about to leave the house, when he heard the phone ring. He rushed back to the living room. It was a private number. He answered the phone. There was silence on the other end.

"Is this Andy?" asked a feeble voice.

"Yes," said Andy recognising the voice of Tsang.

"How are you doing?" enquired Tsang. "I'm fine and you?" replied Andy.

It was the first time both spoke with a formal greeting and a sense of camaraderie which surprised Andy.

"Have you opened the canister?" asked Tsang.

"No, can I open it?" asked Andy seeking permission, feeling confused about his relationship with Tsang. He was being polite when he should be furious for putting him and his family in danger.

"Yes, if you can. In fact, I called you to warn you that they know the artefact has left the country and they may track you down," said Tsang sounding grave.

 Andy's heart was pumping fast and his mind was trying to keep up.

"Who is, "they"?" he asked.

"Chang YinNi. Google his name, but do it from a secure location."

"What's inside in the artefact?" asked Andy quickly, as he didn't want to lose another opportunity to find out from the horse's mouth.

"I don't know. All I know is that only you can open it," replied Tsang.

Andy was disappointed. He was expecting more information from Tsang.

He hesitated and said, "I am going to London in two days."

"Don't leave it anywhere. Take it with you, wherever you go. It's your insurance."

"Got to go, will be in touch," said Tsang hastily and the line went dead.

CHAPTER 52

"You told him, you were going to London! Seriously, what were you even thinking," screamed Cara, hurling cushions at Andy!
"Stop it, will you! Now, be an adult," pleaded Andy.
Cara was livid and wasn't going to be appeased easily. "I should not be having this conversation with you as you are nothing but an irresponsible adult. You don't care about exposing your family to danger."

The kids came running into the living room to witness the drama that was unfolding.
"What happened dad?" enquired Eric?
"Nothing to worry kids. Mum and I are just talking about an incident at work. Why don't you go out cycling?" offered Andy.
The kids were happy to get the extra play time and rushed out at once.

Returning to their conversation, Andy tried to calm Cara down.
"Relax, I trust him. He called to warn me about an impending danger. I did not want him troubling you, especially when I'm in London."
Cara was in no mood to listen to him. "Absolute nonsense! They have cost us enough trouble already. Have you googled the name of the person that you asked?"
"Not yet. He told me to use a secured laptop from a remote Internet connection. I was planning to visit a Cyber Centre in the Downtown area," replied Andy.
"What are you waiting for? Do it now!" yelled Cara. She was fed up with this game and wanted to get rid of the artefact as soon as possible.

On entering the Cyber Centre, Andy occupied the closest workstation.

Quickly opening the browser, he typed Chen YiNi's name and Hong Kong.

The personal profile of Chen YiNi popped up. He went numb. The page showed a picture of a man with a pleasant face, who was a dangerous mobster in all of Asia. He was based out of Hong Kong.

He was shocked by this revelation. Why are these guys after this artefact? How am I involved in all of this?

Cara is going to be livid, he thought.

CHAPTER 53

Chang YiNi was born into a middle-class family. His father was an accountant and his mother had a small store, by the banks of the Victoria Bay. The family was a small and happy one. He finished his schooling in Hong Kong. He was a brilliant student and a topper in school.

Chang was very keen to become an entrepreneur and wanted to start his own auditing company. He had enrolled for Bachelors of Commerce to help him fulfil his dreams.

One day while returning from college, he found a few thugs messing with his mother for some cigarettes. Chang darted to his mum's rescue, but his mum stopped him and ordered him to leave the shop.

The next day morning there was a crowd standing in front of their house. Walking out, he found graffiti on the outer wall of his house. A graffiti by the mob on the walls of a house in Hong Kong meant that they were marked and anyone who dealt with them, were also marked.

As news of the graffiti got around, Chang's dad lost his job and his mother was asked to move out of her shop and the family was issued an eviction notice from their house owner. Chang's father met the house owner and his boss, appealing to them but they would not listen to him. In an act of rage, Chang walked into mob's neighbourhood and quarrelled with him. He was beaten so brutally that he was unable to move for weeks. Unable to cope with the pressure and humiliation, his parents committed suicide.

Chang was never the same again. His life has changed forever. He was inconsolable and vowed revenge. He discontinued his college education and started to work in Shanghai as a cook to stay away from the mob and terrifying memories.

Chang developed his cooking skills and mastered various cuisines. The restaurant was frequented by influential people and Shanghai mafia.

Chang got close to Zhang, the kingpin of Shanghai's business district. He was an elderly man who loved Cantonese food and would visit the restaurant every week. One day he invited Chang and offered him a business deal, to start his own restaurant chain. Chang jumped at the offer and started to build his own chain of restaurants. Within a short time, his business grew leaps and bounds. The food was great and service was excellent. Soon Chang became a celebrated chef and business owner.

One day, Chang contacted Zhang's closest aide and secretly enquired about Zhang's other ventures. He learnt that Zhang controlled the narcotic trade and the mafia business in China. He is a notorious criminal, who was wanted by the authorities in all South Asian countries. Yet, here he was sitting in front of him and having his dinner without a care in the world.

The next day, out of curiosity, Chang checked about Zhang on the internet. There was Interpol Red Alert on his name. But the person in the picture was someone else. This was shocking. So, is Zhang an imposter? He thought.

Chang was troubled by this revelation and wanted to confront Zhang.

He got his chance one late afternoon when Zhang visited his restaurant. The customers had left and just few cleaning staff was around setting tables for dinner. Chang was chatting with Zhang as always, and then he mustered courage and casually asked him about the facial transformation. Zhang's face turned red. He got up from his seat and left the restaurant without a word. Later that evening, Chang was escorted to Zhang's home by his aide. It was a humongous property with a beautiful garden. Zhang received Chang with open arms and offered him a cup of tea. Zhang led him to a study, where there were pictures of his younger years. Chang could see the photos resembled the one he saw on the Internet. Confused, he enquired about his facial transformation.

"I got a plastic surgery done by a trusted friend of mine, who is based in Singapore. He visits me on a weekly basis to check if I'm healing. He is in fact in town and you should meet him." Looking closely, Chang could see a scar under Zhang's chin leading all the way up to his ears. Chang apologised profusely and invited Zhang and his friend for dinner and promise to cook their favourite dishes.

A few days later, he threw a great banquet for the Shanghai underworld to celebrate the success of his restaurant. During dinner, Chang announced that the restaurant chain is launching its first outlet in Hong Kong next week and to celebrate this occasion, a great party was organised for Hong Kong mafia in Macau.

The following week Zhang received shocking news that the entire Hong Kong mafia was poisoned and more than 84 people, including the head of the faction, had died of food poisoning at the party held by Chang. Zhang was shaken. He was trying to digest the news when he received a call from Chang.

"I'm outside, please let me in."

Once in the privacy of his house, Chang explained his motive behind killing the mafia and that he had planned it for a long time to avenge his parent's death. But Zhang was furious that Chang used their business partnership for his personal reason. He signalled his bodyguards to kill Chang. To his surprise, his bodyguards collapsed in front of him. Before he could react, he felt a sharp object cut through his stomach. His eyesight started to fade and darkness set in.

CHAPTER 54

Chang's bodyguard slowly pulled out the dagger out of the lifeless body of Zhang. "What about his friend?" asked Chang. "He's dead in the next room," said the bodyguard. "Good, time to make the announcement." Next day, he gathered the entire Shanghai mafia for an urgent meeting at Zhang's house. None of them knew the reason but sensed some grave purpose.

They were all seated in the main hall and were served tea. Everyone was getting impatiently and started to speculate. Just then, they were all led to the inner courtyard of the house. The entire mob froze at the sight of Zhang's body hanging from the inner balcony. Chang stood in the upper balcony and addressed the mob.

"Welcome everyone. As you can see, I have killed Zhang and all the members of the Hong Kong mafia too."

A few contemplated running up the stairs to attack Chang but they were outnumbered and the bodyguards were alert.

"Who did not have the tea, raise your hands."

None went up.

"Good," said Chang, "Please walk into the inner chamber of the house. We'll talk as brothers."

The mob was completely baffled as to why Chang is interested in knowing if they had tea. As the crowd moved through the door they found a scanner which indicated a green light. People who triggered a red light were led to the next room.

Once they were all inside, Chang appeared in a distance. He was guarded and had a bottle of green liquid in his hand.

"Dear brothers," he addressed. "I am your new leader!"

There was an outburst and people started to advanced towards Chang.

"Before you get violent, please note you have all been poisoned," announced Chang.

The crowd stopped at their feet. They knew Chang was not joking as he has just killed the entire Hong Kong mafia and they would be no exception.

"But the good news is, I have an antidote. I cannot save you, but

I can keep you alive as long as you listen to me."

A few refused to listen and advanced to attack him but were shot down by the guards in the room.

He continued, "The tea you were served was poisoned with a unique substance. Most poisons kill their victims when consumed. This works the other way around. You will all die if you don't consume it every 72 hours!"

CHAPTER 55

Chang ruled with an iron hand. He killed anyone who opposed him. He invented a new drug called 'Green Joy'. He used cocaine along with a poison to create this super drug. This drug was like no other. People who consumed green joy were highly productive and were always in a state of ecstasy. It was the perfect drug but had a deadly flaw. If you stop consuming it, you would be dead within 72 hours. The demand for the drug reached beyond the walls of China and soon the world was his marketplace. Chang became a monster. The years of trauma had changed him forever. He became fearless and detached himself from all human emotions. He was power hungry and there was no stopping this beast.

Andy glanced at his phone. It was Cara. There were 6 missed calls and a tonne of messages. He had been engrossed in reading about Chang and didn't even notice the time.

He dialled Cara. She answered it immediately, "What's going on? It's 11 P.M., I was getting worried."

"Sorry, my phone was on silent. I'm just leaving now and will be home soon," comforted Andy.

He was driving through the busy roads of Dubai. It is a city that never sleeps. There was still traffic on roads. His mind was pre-occupied about how to break the news of Chang in a way that won't scare Cara.

The door was immediately answered by Cara. Anxiously, she asked, "So, what did you find out? Who is he?"

Andy decided that it was futile to cover up and he replied, "He is a dangerous drug dealer and heads the Shanghai Mafia".

There was complete silence and a few minutes later Cara said, "I want to go to my mum's place. I will call my parents and let them know. Once you return from London, we can decide on the next steps."

Andy was expecting a wave of words, but her resigned outlook made him guilty and sad. She didn't sleep well that night and first thing in the morning, pulled out the suitcases and asked the kids to start packing. Andy sat in the living room overcome by the feeling of helplessness.

Cara's parents lived in Dubai, not far from them. Her dad worked for the local Airlines as Operations Director and was due to retire in 2 year's time. Her mum was a headmistress for a renowned school for special needs children. Having them in close proximity was a great help for Cara and Andy in raising their children.

The artefact has turned their life upside down and now, his kids and wife were moving away from him. He decided to call his dad to update him and seek his advice.

Andy informed about Chang and that Cara was leaving with the Kids to her mum's.

Ted listened intently and spoke after few minutes of introspection.

"I think it's better Cara leaves to her mum's, or you can bring them to London with you and they can stay with us while you finish your work. But staying back in Dubai will not affect Cara's work or children's school. I'm sure Cara will feel better and safe at her mum's," advised Ted.

Andy thanked him for his support and bid goodbye.

He then went into the bedroom and saw Cara packing. He held her tightly and could feel her tears drop on his shoulders.

"I am sorry. I should have listened to you and distanced myself from this whole affair. I promise to put an end to this matter soon."

Cara quietly withdrew and renewed her packing. Andy felt sick in the stomach. He had expected her to react strongly, but her actions drove a spike through his heart.

He dropped off Cara and kids in the evening to his in-law's place. Heading back home, he distracted himself from drowning in misery by preparing for his trip to London. He called his cousins to inform them about his itinerary.

Next morning, he was picked up by his company car to take him to the airport.

At the Airport, he saw Tony by the check-in counter.

"Have you checked-in?" enquired Andy.

"Yes, did it online last evening. I had a lot of luggage and thought best to check in early."

Once on the flight, Andy buckled the seat belt and waited for the flight to take off.

"You look tensed, everything ok?" enquired Tony.

"All good, just tensed about the expo. It was a late decision to participate and I am not sure if the preparation has been thorough," replied Andy.

"Well you better, I am not going to be around to cover your back, mate. I just put down my papers. I resigned yesterday, so you, my friend are the new Director of Sales, Congratulations!"

CHAPTER 56

Andy was speechless.

"Hey, you look like you have seen a ghost! I know we get along well, but I never thought you will be upset with my resignation. I am happy to have a colleague like you," quipped Tony.

Andy smiled and tried to behave normally. He was stunned at the prediction of the monk. There was a flood of questions in his mind. How could have the monk predict this event so accurately? Everything was fine with Tony until yesterday. So what prompted him to resign? Did Omar and Tony have a fall out?

He decided to clear the suspense, "Why, the sudden decision?" enquired Andy.

"It's purely a personal one. I have been away from my folks in London and my dad needs help. He will be turning 80 next year. Secondly, my daughter has decided to pursue her college in London," explained Tony.

"Don't worry buddy, you will be fine. If you need me, I'm just a phone call away," assured Tony.

"Thanks, Tony! I will really miss you, buddy. Good luck for the next chapter in your life" wished Andy.

Andy opened a book to read but mind was elsewhere. He was thinking that in a corporate environment, there is a fair share of surprises and developments each day. It seemed like the universe had conspired to provide Andy with the promotion and it was predicted accurately a month ago. The pieces of the puzzle which made this moment a reality required Tony's daughter to obtain college admission in London. He could have arranged campus accommodation for his daughter or could have asked her to stay with the grandparents. What if she was not admitted in London? Instead, she was offered an opportunity in the US or she could have continued her studies in Dubai.

Secondly, Tony's father was old but did not require urgent attention. He was comfortable and did not require any immediate medical attention. Tony himself could have dismissed the idea, as he was well settled in Dubai with a great tax-free package. It all fell into place like a jigsaw puzzle in the correct sequence.

CHAPTER 57

At Heathrow airport, Andy and Tony parted ways. Both had refused hotel accommodation provided by their office, as they wanted to stay with their respective families.

Andy walked out of the arrival building to find his cousins waiting. "Andy!" shouted his cousin Jerry and ran up to him, closely followed by Ryan. After the usual exchange of pleasantries, they took the tube to Swiss Cottage, where Andy's parents lived.

"I see you have travelled light. We can now go directly to the pub for a drink," suggested Jerry slyly. Andy was too knackered to join them, but he thought it was impossible to talk these madcaps out of it.

Two pints down, not wanting to be fagged, Andy directed his cousins to the dark corner. After ordering for some chips, they retired with a Cuban cigar. Andy gave his cousins a rundown of the events. Both listened intently and finally, Jerry broke out "It's an amazing adventure waiting to happen. I can take some days off from work."

"Same here, I am not missing this for the world," pitched in Ryan.

"Great, I have to first finish the expo and then we can meet Nick's dad to decipher the script," said Andy.

"That settles it. We will all meet at Nick's tomorrow evening," added Jerry excitedly.

CHAPTER 58

Andy joined Jerry and Rayan after having spent the last hour updating his dad and mum about life in Dubai.

Nick opened the door and could smell the booze. Nick blurted out, "Assholes, you went to the pub without me."

"Sorry bro, couldn't resist a beautiful tavern on our way here," apologised Andy, while giving Nick a hug.

"I can see you guys have been up to no good, nothing changes," taunted Nick exchanging hugs with his cousins.

"Calm down. Where is your feeding bottle? Let me get this baby some milk," teased Ryan.

Nick was the youngest of all the cousins and frequently the butt of jokes and pranks.

Nick's dad, Michael, entered the living room from his study after hearing the commotion. He was a tall lanky man with grey hair and extremely fit for his age. He was an expert in the field of Linguistics and much-respected scholar in England.

He greeted the boys and enquired about their life in general. Nick's mum, Nancy, who was busy in kitchen cooking dinner, also joined them.

"I'm heading over to the store to pick up some wine. Do you fellas need anything? There is beer in the fridge. Help yourself," said Michael.

Nancy gave a stern look at Michael and said "Wine? Mister, you remember the doctor has advised you cut down on your drinking. Go easy!" scolded Nancy.

By the time, she finished her sentence, Michael was out of earshot.

The boys let out a chuckle and Nancy went back to the kitchen, muttering angrily. They settled down with the beer and waited for Michael to return.

Michael returned in time for Dinner. Nancy had set up the table and smell of mince pies was filling the room. They hogged like they hadn't eaten for days and polished off the custard in a jiffy.

They all moved to the backyard for a smoke and lounged in the Gazebo. The weather was warm with clear skies and a bright moon was visible.

"I need your help, Uncle Mike," said Andy. Andy relayed everything about the artefact and Tsang . He showed him photos and videos which he had on his phone.

Michael printed some of these pictures using the Wi-Fi printer and rushed into his study to fetch them. An hour had passed and there was no sign of him. "What's keeping him so long?" asked Andy

"Don't worry. I am sure he is working on the photos. The wine bottle is still here, so he has not dozed off. If not for us, he has to come out to get the wine," laughed Nick, while others just stared at him. "He is behind me, right?" guessed Nick. Michael gave a light knock on his head and said, "You are right. I came here for the wine, but I see you fellas have downed it."

The others cracked up watching Nick's mortified face.

CHAPTER 59

Michael sat back in his chair and made himself comfortable, then began with his explanation.

"The script used was from the Mauryan era. The Mauryan Empire was founded by Emperor Chandragupta Maurya which dominated ancient India between c. 322 and 187 BCE. Originating from the kingdom of Magadha, in the Indo-Gangetic Plain in the eastern side of the Indian subcontinent, the empire had its capital city at Pataliputra (modern day Patna). The empire was the largest to have ever existed in the Indian subcontinent, spanning over 5 million square kilometres at its zenith under Emperor Asoka.

Emperor Chandragupta Maurya raised an army and with the assistance of Chanakya, overthrew the Nanda Empire in c. 322 BCE and rapidly expanded his power westwards by taking advantage of the disruptions in western India caused by Alexander the Great's armies. By 316 BCE the empire had fully occupied Northwestern India.

The great Empire stretched to the north along the natural boundaries of the Himalayas, to the east into Assam, to the west into Balochistan (south-west Pakistan and south-east Iran) and the Hindu Kush mountains of what is now Afghanistan."

Michael paused for a while and looked at all of them listening so raptly. He was satisfied to see none had fallen asleep. He then continued, "The script on the artefact is a secret code that was used only by the generals of King Asoka. The scripts were found in one of the archaeological sites in India. The person who etched the script onto the artefact had to be a General, who was in the core group of Asoka's army."

Andy relived the visions where the warrior was sitting in the pool of blood.

"The problem is, I only have part of the code, as most of the scriptures were destroyed with time. But I can reconstruct the words if I can see the entire writings on the artefact. Do you have more pictures?" asked Michael.

"Still better, I have the artefact," said Andy gleaming. Despite his promise to Cara, Andy had opted to carry the artefact as it was the only insurance against Chang. He knew it did not raise any flags during their return from Hong Kong. So he had tucked it into his suitcase knowing fully well that it will not glow until there was visual contact.

CHAPTER 60

Andy had carefully covered the artefact in a red satin pouch and had placed it in the inner sleeve of his jacket. He pulled it out and placed it on the table. There was a bright light beaming from the canister more so in the dimly lit Gazebo. Michael and the others were speechless and mesmerised by the sheer beauty of the object. Finally, Andy broke the silence, "So, what do you make of it?"

"It's amazing! I have not seen or heard of anything like this during my years at the university," said Michael, unable to withdraw eye from the artefact. Andy told them about what he had heard from Julius, the jeweller and the metal that glows. He then gently turned the artefact to project the writings on the garden wall.

Michael ran into his study to collect his code book and his diary to take notes. The code was complex, wherein most of the alphabets looked the same and since he had only part of the script, Michael had to improvise to crack the message.

After a few minutes, they had deciphered two words, "I am". Jerry suggested we move on and try to decipher the small words first, then try to crack the big ones. An hour later, Michael had made little progress. They only had the sentence-"I am ....open...." "This is stange, the name quoted is the same as the one giving the instructions." said Michael.

After taking a long and hard look at it, the team found themselves frustrated and tired. Andy then decided to share the details of his dreams, hoping for some clues to be unearthed.

"The scene you described could be the war of Kalinga and if you think the person you saw was a general, I can dig up the names of Asoka's generals who were with him during the war. We could insert the names and see what happens," suggested Michael.

"Absolute Tosh! Dad, do you really think it can hear what we say?" inquired Nick.

"Based on what Andy has told us so far, I believe so. Now if you excuse me, I have work to do," said Michael rushing off to his den.

The team had moved into the living room and were watching the re-runs.

A couple of hours had passed before Michael returned with a list, which had the names of generals who fought alongside Asoka, scribbled in an obscure paper, which only Michael could understand.

Michael instructed Andy to place the artefact on the table and call out one by one the general names. He started with a first name 'Turasara'. He spoke in a distinct voice "I am Turasara, open Turasara". Everyone waited with bated breath. But there was no change in the artefact. Then one by one, Andy repeated the sentence using all names from the list, but nothing happened. Disappointed and exhausted, the team crashed out for the night.

CHAPTER 61

Andy felt a strange sensation like someone was watching him. Opening his eyes, he saw Michael staring at him from the far side of the living room with a cup of coffee. It took Andy a while to realise that he was at Nick's house and that he had crashed out on the couch last night. Suddenly, Michael jumped from the chair almost spilling his coffee and bolted to his study. Ryan and Jerry were nowhere to be found, while Nick had plunked on the floor in his sleeping bags. He headed over to Michael's study and greeted him.

"Good morning Andy. The blokes have gone to get us breakfast as Nancy is busy packing. She's off to attend her nephew's wedding in Northampton. It will be nice and quiet here. We can get some work done," quipped Michael.

He continued with some seriousness, "I have done some research, based on your dreams and the timeline of the script. In the fierce war of Kalinga, none of Asoka's general survived except Turasara. All the other generals were killed in the war. Turasara and Asoka then converted to Buddhism and left the country in the hands of his son and daughter.

"Why don't we consider Asoka? What if this was his handiwork?" proposed Andy.

"It's a possibility. I was also thinking along the lines of using their Buddhist names," replied Michael. Devanm Priya was Ashoka's and Nirvanpali, Turasara's.

Immediately, Andy picked up the artefact and spoke: "I am Ashoka, Open Ashoka".

Nothing happened. Let me try the next one. "I am Turasara, open Turasara," still nothing. But this time, Andy felt a slight vibration.

"It just vibrated like a cell phone. I must have missed it yesterday, as it's very subtle," said Andy shivering with excitement.

"Try it again," coaxed Michael.

"I am Turasara, open Turasara," and there was a distinct buzz but nothing more.

"Should we try his Buddhist name?" asked Andy.

"His Buddhist name was Nirvanpali, meaning attainer of Nirvana," replied Michael.

"I am Nirvanapali, open Nirvanapali," echoed Andy.

Instantly, the artefact was illuminated with a bright luminescent particle and with a violent vibration it split into two.

CHAPTER 62

Andy was groggy and was yo-yoing between reality and hallucination. After focussing hard, he realised he was lying on the back seat of the car. The car was speeding through the streets of central London. Nick was at the wheel and next to him was Michael, frantically instructing him to the British Memorial Hospital. Glancing back, he saw Jerry and Ryan crouching in the boot peering into their mobile phones. "Hey fellas, where are we going? How did I get into the car? I don't remember a thing" Nick jammed the brakes and pulled over.

"How are you feeling?" enquired Michael with a mixed feeling of relief and worry.

"You were knocked out after the artefact opened. A light went straight into your body," informed Michael.

"We tried to revive you, but you were not responding. So, we decided to take you to the hospital," added Jerry.

"I am feeling fine. Just a little dizzy," assured Andy.

"Now that you are conscious, let's go to the hospital and get you checked. We don't have to give them any specific reason. Just a general check-up should do," instructed Michael.

45 minutes later, Andy walked out of the observation room.

"Anything to worry about?" asked Jerry.

"I don't know," said Andy still groggy.

The doctor who examined Andy approached them. She was blond, tall, slim and spoke with a deep confident tone.

"Your reports seem to be fine. Since the alcohol level in your blood is beyond admissible limits, I cannot comment on the blood test. Overall everything is normal except for the burn mark on your chest. It looks

like someone put a hot one pound coin on your chest,"
informed the doctor.

"How did it happen?" she asked.

Andy unbuttoned his shirt and tried to get a look at it but the burn was just below his neck. Michael lent him to a mirror. The area felt coarse when he ran his fingers across it but there was no sensation. The guys took turns observing the mark and Jerry examined Andy's back but there was nothing there. "Whatever it is, my dear cousin, is inside you," he whispered.

The Doctor continued, "I am Dr.Linda, the duty doctor. My number is 4467689789. You can reach me anytime, if you have any queries or if you feel ill. I have listed a set of medicines that will heal the burn."

"Hello, Linda. I am Ryan and I always wanted to be a Doctor," Ryan was trying his pickup line.

"I am sure, we will have some queries," added Jerry.

"Unbelievable!" muttered Nick and Andy smiled coyly as they exited the Hospital.

CHAPTER 63

All of them crammed into the car feeling relieved that Andy was alright.

Andy phone rang and it was his dad. Michael had informed him about the incident. Andy appraised his dad of his condition and promised to look after himself and not be foolhardy.

As soon as he hung up, his mind had focussed back to the artefact.

"Was there anything else in the artefact?" he asked.

"Yes. There was a cloth, and it had some diagram on it. I did not get a good look at it as you collapsed. I put it in the study safe." said Michael.

"I'm famished. Let's stop by a restaurant for brunch," announced Jerry.

They stopped at a French Café that surprisingly served English breakfast and beer. Andy ordered a Lager. Jerry and Ryan opted for draught beer and Michael ordered their house wine. The Brunch was set menu, which included Salad, Bacon, Eggs, toast, baked beans, hash browns, pudding, the entire works.

Andy took a sip of the beer and put it back with a disgusted look. Jerry who was halfway through looked surprised. "It's your favourite brand," he said.

"Maybe, it's just the episode," added Andy in his defence.

"Are you suggesting that you might quit drinking, ludicrous! Please order another one," quipped Nick.

"Stop it, you silly oaf!" scolded Michael.

Once they reached home, Michael headed for the study and bought out the artefact and the cloth that was inside it. The design on the cloth was a complicated. It had a concentration of circles, rectangles and triangles. It was weaved with gold and silver thread. There was no writing but the cloth itself was red in colour. The material was unidentifiable. It was made with a metal which was weaved to make a cloth, yet it was supple and flexible. The artefact no longer glowed when Andy was near it. He stared at the diagram on the cloth for a long time and then he suddenly jumped up. "It's an optical illusion, look," he turned the cloth sideways and the cloth turned into a map.

CHAPTER 64

They all gathered around and took turns to look at the map.

"I have seen many hidden messages in pictures and paintings but never one on a cloth and that too with Gold thread. It must have taken the artist ages to do this, and how did he visualise the image while weaving it? Evidently, it was done in layers to create the perfect illusion," said Michael in complete awe of the craftsmanship.

The map was beautiful it depicted mountains, rivers and valleys with amazing precession. But there were no landmarks or any markings pointing to the location. "This could be anywhere in the world," sulked Michael.

"We need to look closer. Going by the story so far it has to be part of the Mauryan Empire, but where?" questioned Michael.

"The Himalayas, where else could you find such mountains," replied Andy.

"The Mauryans did not go that far. Their Empire stopped with Kapilvastu in the north, unless someone went further up North into the Himalayas and to do what? It is impossible to locate this place using this map."

Just then Andy blurted, "I think I have seen this place. I had a dream of sitting on a ledge and I think it was here," he pointed to a spot on the map.

"We have advanced Geo-mapping satellite access in the university. We use it for exploration and site mapping. The computer has Geo maps from all parts of the globe. I will make a copy of this map and run a search for a match," informed Michael.

20 minutes later, Michael left for the University. Ryan and Nick took over the Kitchen to make supper, while

Jerry went out to get some beer. Andy sat glued to the couch waiting for Michael.

At 8:30 P.M., the doorbell rang and Andy bolted towards the door to usher Michael inside. Everyone gathered around him and he stood with a wide grin on his face.

"Got it," he said, plopping himself on the couch. "It's in the Himalayas, 110 kilometres from Kathmandu!"

CHAPTER 65

The next two agonising days were spent looking after the booth at the Expo.

Andy was feeling like he was held captive against his wishes. Finally, when it was over, he bid goodbye to Tony and promised to catch up soon.

He left the convention centre and headed straight to Nick's house.

The living room looked like an adventure store with climbing equipment, rucksacks, package of food and water spread all over the living room.

Michael was busy in the study making calls to his contacts in Kathmandu to arrange for the expedition. Later, the group met over the dinner table.

"We have everything in place, dad has arranged for the Sherpas and guides to take us into the mountains. We have all the supplies for 15 days in the wilderness. Most of this will be shipped today so that the Sherpas can transport part of the items to camp two," updated Nick.

"I have booked the tickets and have obtained the permits from the Government of Nepal for the expedition," informed Jerry.

"I have to call Cara. I have kept her in the dark," thought Andy to himself.

"Uncle Mike, are you sure you are up to this?" enquired Andy.

"Of course, I would not miss this for the world. This could be one of the greatest archaeological discoveries of the century."

They spent the next two day's in getting all the equipment, supplies and paperwork in place.

Andy sat closing his eyes in the Heathrow Airport lobby waiting for the boarding call. Michael walked over and asked "Did you inform anyone of our mission? I just got a call from the university. Someone named Chang was there looking for you."

CHAPTER 66

Fifteen minutes later, the group was sitting with a glum look in the airport coffee shop.

"I can't believe you did this to us. You have misled us from the beginning. Is this all or is there anything else that you're not telling us," asked Michael.

"I promise. This is it," said Andy embarrassed and guilty of leading them into the danger zone.

"You should have at least told us so that we could have made the right choice," said Jerry.

"I did not want to scare you guys. Now seriously, would have you guys come to Nepal if you knew about Chang," replied Andy.

"That's not for you to decide, Andy," shouted Ryan.

"You withheld information and put all of us are in grave danger. If Chang was at the University, then he already knows about your plan. He knows we are travelling to Kathmandu. I'm worried about what is waiting for us when we land in Nepal," said Michael in a hazy tone.

"This trip is going all to pot. You can still back out, you know," said Andy regrettably.

Nick whacked his head from the back, "Are you off, your rockers? I would not miss this adventure because of Chang. What say, guys?"

"No way, mate," said Jerry

"I'm in too because we are mad as a bag of ferrets," laughed Ryan.

"We are not backing out now," said Michael with a smile. "I am in too but you better not throw any more surprises."

"I promise, you know everything now."

Final call for the flight to Kathmandu blasted from the speaker. The group left for the boarding area. They settled into their seats and Andy sent a last-minute email and a few SMS to his friends. Michael was reading the flight manual and Nick was playing a video game on his phone. Andy was just about to close his eyes when the phone rang. It was a private number. Andy answered it immediately.

"You have something we need," said a voice from the other side. "It is in your best interest to hand it over to my contact in Kathmandu. When you exit the airport, you will see a man in blue suit holding a placard stating, Welcome Mr. Simon. You can hand it over to him. If you fail to comply, you and your friends will be dead within 24 hrs."

"Who is this? I have no idea what you're talking about," replied Andy.

"I don't have time for your games. Just do as you're told,"

Before Andy could reply the phone went dead.

Andy quickly shared the details of the phone call with the team. "Evidently, he does not know your name but has your phone number that means Tsang has not told them everything about you. Switch off your phone and let's take a chance and walk past the guy at the airport. But then, who was the guy who came to the university looking for you?" asked Michael.

"Have you told Tsang anything about me?"

"I just told him I was in London. So, who is the guy that called me?" wondered Andy.

"Don't tell me there are two of them now and we don't even know who the second guy is," whispered Nick.

CHAPTER 67

"Let's think this through on the flight," said Michael. Andy went back to his seat but was unable to make sense of what was happening. Tsang had warned him this would happen, but then who is the second caller? If Chang was in London, why would he come on his own? It's too risky and how did he get into the country, as he is one of the most wanted criminals in the world. Andy spent the next few hours recollecting all the instances, but could not make sense of the situation.

He gave up and soon went into a deep slumber. He found himself in a royal court surrounded by fierce-looking generals carrying deadly weapons and peering over a map of a treacherous region. Asoka the great presented his strategy to win the war and the generals shared their thoughts. Asoka then enquired his generals about their unit and gave his orders to be carried out.

"Andy, Wake up! We have landed in Kathmandu," came Jerry's voice as he pulled him out of the dream. Kathmandu is the capital city of the Federal Democratic Republic of Nepal, the largest Himalayan state in Asia. It is the largest metropolis in Nepal, with a population of 1.4 million in the city proper, and 5 million across the Kathmandu Valley, which includes the towns of Lalitpur, Kirtipur, Madhyapur Thimi and Bhaktapur. Kathmandu is also the largest metropolis in the Himalayan hill region.

The team got down from the plane and were ushered into the lobby area. As Andy headed towards the immigration clearance counter, a lean man with a shaved head in a uniform asked him if he needed any help. Andy quickly instructed him that the team was tired and they would like to avoid waiting at customs and bypass the long queue.

"No problem Sir. I will assist you," said the officer whose nameplate read Thimpu Narang. He led them to a VIP counter where the customs check was done immediately.

They also requested Thimpu, if he could arrange airport taxi to take them to their hotel. A couple of phone calls later, they were taken to a parking lot where a minivan was stationed. They jumped into the van and sped towards Kathmandu city.

They had escaped, but for how long?

CHAPTER 68

The drive through the city was exciting. The landscape was captivating with towering mountains overlooking the busy central market. Most of the snow caps had melted except at the top. The summertime is ideal for trekkers and climbers. There were a lot of tourists on the streets.

Andy missed Cara and the kids. They would have loved this place, he thought.

His heart was heavy after he spoke to Cara from London just before he left to Kathmandu. He told her about the expedition. She was livid and screamed at him for keeping her in the dark. At the same time, she was missing him so badly and wanted this nightmare to end soon. She was desperate to go back to her home and reclaim their happy life. She choked with emotion before she hung up.

Andy requested the driver to stop for breakfast. The group went to a hotel and had a heavy breakfast of momos. Michael instructed the team to get the gear from the car and head out to the meeting point. The driver was having a cigarette and was surprised when the team collected their belongings, "What happened, anything wrong?" quizzed the driver.

"Sorry, there is a change of plans," said Andy handing him 100-dollar bill. The driver was elated, "Thank you, sir. You are very generous."

The team made their way through the winding streets and crowded places of Kathmandu to the designated guide's office.

"Welcome to Kathmandu!" shouted a short and lean chap in his 30's. He proceeded to give Michael a bear hug. After an exchange of pleasantries, Michael announced. "This is Bishal Karki, an Expedition

Expert. I have had the opportunity to use his expertise couple of times for my research. He is a climber's dream come true and a specialist in local culture and region."

They all shook hands with him and introduced themselves.

"We have everything ready, Michael. When would you like to leave?"

"Excellent, we leave today."

Perplexed by the sudden request Bishal asked, "But, you have just landed. Don't you want to rest for a day or two to climatize?"

"We are in a hurry Bishal, we leave today," said Michael.

CHAPTER 69

At 4 P.M., the entire team crammed themselves in the minivan along with 2 guides and 4 sherpas. Since Michael had already sent the resources and tools ahead of time, they could travel light. The location was to the south of Kathmandu. The team would travel by road to a place called Himshi and from here, there would go on foot to the silent valley.
Silent Valley got its name due to the lack of noise. It was a natural rock formation that made this valley an echo-proof zone. The place was a favourite for hermits, who stayed in the natural caves here to pray and meditate. The tributary of river Trishuli ran through the valley.

As dusk fell, the party reached Himshi, a small village on the banks of river Trishuli. There were numerous camps set up by Bishal that were ready for occupancy. Each member was given a separate tent and there was a common toilet and bath. Dinner was being prepared by the Sherpas. It was a mix of rice, soup, fried chicken and baked potatoes. The team retired early as they were tired and had an early start next day. The trek to the silent valley would take three days by foot a total of 56km through treacherous terrain.

CHAPTER 70

Andy woke up to the sound of the alarm. It was 5:30 A.M. The cold frigid air tempted him back to the comfort of the sleeping bag, but he forced himself out of bed and peeped out. It was dark but he could already see a lot of activity at the camp. The sherpas were strapping the gear and were preparing to leave. The guides were having their breakfast and Michael was checking his GPS and other equipment. Andy slipped into his gear and walked up to Michael, who was helping himself with a hot cup of coffee and a piece of bread. Michael handed him some whisky to mix with the coffee. "It will keep you warm, rub some on your feet."

"Where are the boys?" enquired Andy.

"Fast asleep, but that is least of our problems. Did you realise something about the map? Firstly, it does not have any location names and secondly, what are we supposed to find in the valley?" pondered Michael.

"True. We found this place because of the Geo-mapping computer at the University and the X mark indicated here, is a big mountain. It could take us ages to find the exact spot. I am only hoping that once we are there the signs would lead us to it."replied Andy.

"We will need some luck out there," said Michael with a hint of pessimism.

By 7 A.M., everyone was ready and the party started the three-day trek to the silent valley.

The driver who picked Andy and the team from the airport was tied to a chair and there was blood dripping from a deep gash in his forehead.

"For the last time, where did you drop the foreigners?" asked a man in English. "I am telling you the truth. They gave me USD 100 and left by foot from the restaurant. I don't know where they went. Please believe me."

"Contact all the agents in the city. I want to know where they went."

CHAPTER 71

The party trekked into the wilderness. The climate got cooler as they left the city and slowly the nature around them changed. The tree line started to decrease and as they moved on, the vegetation thinned.

By nightfall, the party were relieved to see the tents set up. The sherpas were sent ahead to set up the entire infrastructure for the group. "The expedition is very well organised," said Andy pleased with the arrangements.

"These guys are professionals," said Michael.

"They organise treks to Everest every year and Bishal has been in the business for a decade. I first met him in China, when we were exploring the early Mongolian civilisations that existed and needed an expert to guide us. He was very resourceful. We had to fly him down from Kathmandu, but it was worth it. He is also an expert tracker and his people have been trained in this skill. The Sherpas in his team are honest and hardworking bunch, who will sacrifice themselves but will not let any harm come your way. They are very loyal and treat their guests as God."

"Glad to know, we are in safe hands," said Jerry.

"Look," pointed Ryan towards a distance. "I think I saw a light in the mountains."

"Looks like another party," said Andy peering through his binoculars.

The guides joined them by now. One of them, Gagan said "Strange! I am sure there is no other party authorised to trek in these parts. I saw the schedule and we were the only party allowed in the valley. The Government regulates the number of expeditions to conserve the ecology."

Michael immediately asked Gagan to check with Bishal using the satellite phone. The group gathered around Gagan as he placed the call but there was no answer on the office number or on his mobile.

"Call his house," said Michael to the surprise of the Gagan. There was a woman's voice on the other side. She sounded hysterical and scared. After a brief exchange of words, Gagan disconnected the call."

That was Bishal's sister-in-law. "He was found dead this morning outside his office. He was brutally tortured before he met his end."

CHAPTER 72

They all stood speechless. Each of them was trying to internalise the real danger they are in and think of an action plan to save themselves. The Guides and Sherpas meanwhile joined hands and prayed for their employer's soul to rest in peace. They wept as he was more like their big brother.

"We have to leave now," said Michael to Gagan with a sense of urgency.
He was confused.
"What's the hurry, let's stick to the plan."
Michael explained to him that the party behind them were dangerous people and is looking out for them. They may have also even killed Bishal.
Not quite synthesising the information, he continued to protest "It is very dangerous in the dark and apart from that we need to pack and let the Sherpas get a head start."
"How far do you think the party behind is?"
"Less than a day, I guess. They are really fast."
"I don't care about the danger. If we stay here, we are dead anyways," said Andy
"Let the sherpas wrap up and catch up to us. Let's get a head start. Now move it," instructed Jerry.

The team strapped on headlights and carried a torch each. A rope line was tied between all to keep them in line. The cold mist swept in and the visibility was almost nil. The sherpas handed out oxygen cylinder to prevent dizziness due to the altitude.
As the team moved along the ridges, there was cracking sound followed by a tug on the rope. The team was rapidly retreating into the crevasse below. Andy was the first to fall over. Jerry followed but Gagan was quick to insert the clamp into the ground

and asked everyone to do the same. Michael managed to clamp himself in time. Ryan managed to grab the rock surface and quickly inserted his clamp. Jerry and Andy followed, and they gradually began to climb upwards.

Andy looked down to find Nick's body dangling by the rope. He shouted out to Gagan and explained the situation. He instructed Andy to cut the rope that connected him to Ryan and get to safety. Once both Jerry and Ryan were safe, Gagan asked Andy to hook the clamps, so it can hold their weight.

To Andy's surprise, a second rope dropped next to him and found Gagan rappelling down. A few minutes later Gagan set up a temporary pad to hoist Nick. In the meantime, Michael had set up a pulley to hoist Nick to safety.

"All set. Pull," shouted Gagan. Gradually Nick was raised to safety. Andy and Gagan followed and were finally back on solid ground. Gagan checked Nick's pulse and announced, "He is alive. I think he passed out without enough oxygen. The exhaustion due to lack of climatization could have also played a role. I think we should rest till day break."

"No, we cannot," said Michael pointing to the lights in the distance.

"It's our sherpas," protested Gagan.

"Look behind them," said Andy. There was a second cluster of lights catching up with the first group.

"They are really fast. Half a day maximum," yelled Gagan.

He pulled out the oxygen mask and placed it over Nick's face and injected him with a thermal injection to increase his body temperature. 30 minutes later, Nick opened his eyes and before he could move there was a hand on his shoulder.

"Are you fine, mate?" inquired Jerry in a concerned voice.

"What happened? My head hurts."
"You passed out and took all of us with you into the crevasse," teased Ryan.

Gagan examined Nick and was convinced that he was good to go. He strapped him to the centre of the pack to prevent any further incidents and they restarted their ascend.

At dawn, they were in sight of the silent valley.
"There it is," pointed Gagan looking exhausted. "We should be there by afternoon. Any specific place you want to visit?"
"That one, the one that looks like a horse's head," pointed Michael.
They took a short break. Michael opened the map, calculated the coordinates to ensure they were on the right track.
 "The sherpas are not here. Any idea about their location?" asked Jerry.
"I tried contacting them on the radio but did not get through. We only have supplies to reach the Horsehead and if the sherpas don't turn up we cannot make it back!" said Gagan with a worried look.

CHAPTER 73

The silent valley was spellbinding. The panoramic view of the place was so magical, that you feel like, you are in a different dimension. The vibrant colours of the flowers, the aroma, the sound of birds and butterflies made the whole experience surreal. The flora and fauna was abundant. The Valley was an oasis with an ecosystem of its own and boasted an amazing diversity of plants and trees.

The entire team was soaking in its beauty, when Gagan said, "The hermits bought the plants here and over the centuries this place has become completely self-sufficient. You can stay here and the land will provide everything for you."

"Please leave meat and alcohol here, as it's not allowed in the valley."

There was a loud whine from the team. "Alcohol too, it's a life saver," pleaded Jerry.

"Trust me you won't need it," added Gagan. The party entered the valley and there was absolute silence.

"There is heavy deposits of Amethyst on the floor and black tourmaline in the surrounding mountains which are conducive for meditation and to enhance the creative powers. The black tourmaline acts as a protection by not allowing negativity to enter the valley. The mountains bordering the valley have large deposits of black tourmaline and the valley bed is made of amethyst."

Gagan took his axe and smacked the ground and small fragments of rock crystals sprung out. Cleaning them with fresh water he handed it over to Andy. It was Amethyst.

By noon, the party finally arrived at the horse face. They assembled their climbing gear and set out to climb up the mountain.

"Where exactly do you want to go?" asked Gagan with a puzzled look on his face.

Andy pointed to a ledge just below the shape that looked like a horse nose. The climb was surprisingly gradual.

"I expected a challenge," quipped Nick. As the team turned the corner, the path ended abruptly with a steep 90-degree climb to the top.

"I hope you are happy now," sneered Ryan. All members had rock climbing pedigree. Andy and Jerry were free climbers, but Gagan offered to climb first to drill the clamps and lead the way for the others. Nick was stationed to guard the gear and warn them if Chang's team shows up. The climb was very technical as the rock face allowed very little cracks for Gagan to get a grip.

The team followed the route suggested by Gagan and they reached the top of the mountain but were unable to descend into the ledge below. The only way was to climb down using a rope but since the ledge was a few feet inward they had to swing and land on the platform. Any mistake and a free fall of 300 feet awaited the climbers.

"I will go first," volunteered Andy.

"I prefer Gagan to be there just in case disaster strikes. He can assist us to safety." proposed Jerry

"Let's not be in a hurry. Give me 10 minutes to look for an alternative path," requested Gagan.

"I am sure there is another way," interrupted Andy.

"This whole place is surprisingly familiar to me. It's like I have been to this region before."

20 minutes later, the team was unsuccessful in finding an alternative route and Michael was getting impatient. "I am sorry Andy, but we are running out of time. I am afraid you have to take the risk and jump onto the ledge."

Gagan briefed him on what needs to be done, and Andy slowly held the rope that was tied firmly to a rock and went over the edge. He gradually climbed down to find himself a good 6 feet from the ledge. He took a deep breath and took a couple of swings to build the momentum. He unhooked the clamp and jumped!

CHAPTER 74

Landing perfectly on the ledge, Andy scampered to his feet and looked at the view below. The valley was filled with life force. It was the earth, in a nutshell, all the five elements; earth, water, air, fire and wood all interacted to produce a beautiful valley. Andy sat there mesmerised as the place was familiar. He was home at last! He looked back and found the cave. There was a mat made of cloth in the centre and in the corner a bed made of leaves. To the far-right, there was a small box. He could see the glow under the dust. It was coming from the crack in the rock.

Andy pushed but nothing happened. He then used the clamp, but it would not budge. He went over to the ledge and asked the others to come down. One by one, they successfully landed on the ledge and moved into the small cave.

Andy showed them the crack from which a light was emitting. It was like the glow from the artefact.

"Say the lines you used to open the artefact," advised Michael.

"I am Nirvanpali, open Nirvanpali," said Andy. Suddenly the Rock opened with a loud crack. The stone slab cracked and fell to the ground revealing a manuscript. A bright light flashed from the book and seared straight into Andy's chest.

It was dark when Andy woke up. The group was crouching over the manuscript. "Where is Gagan?" asked Andy, the minute he came to his senses.

"We sent him to get Nick," said Michael.

"So now, no one cares what happens to me?"

"Well you have been struck by lightning before and, we are getting used to it. It's kind of fun to see you fall to the ground," laughed Jerry.

"Come on over great Turasara," invited Michael

"You are the incarnation of the great general-turned-monk," beamed Michael.

"This book is written in the same script. I managed to crack the letter you had written for yourself," declared Michael proudly.

"What are you talking about? How can I be an incarnation of Turasara and why did I leave a message for myself?" asked Andy, baffled and still reeling from the shock.

"That's what this book appears to teach. How to live one lifetime after another. A continuous way for the soul to progress through life, birth, death and rebirth. Turasara had found a way to connect the dots. A way for the soul to remember what it did in its last life and to continue where you left off. Imagine the power one would possess, if you can start where you left and continue what you were seeking. The eternal road for the soul to grow and learn without the hindrance of birth and death. Its knowledge transfer over many lifetimes."

It was too much for Andy to digest. He was still dazed to understand the gravity of the discovery they have made.

"That's why Tsang did not want it to fall into the wrong hands. A tyrant can return to continue torturing the innocent. A thief can hide his ill-gotten wealth and recover it in his next life. A murderer or serial killer can continue creating havoc. The world would be a horrible place and there would be no value for good deeds, as people have nothing to fear, for there will always be a second chance," mumbled Andy.

"We must destroy it. This manuscript will unleash evil and cause many deaths," said Ryan.

"No way. I cannot let you do that," shouted Michael.

"The knowledge in the book is unsurpassable and nothing on this magnitude has ever been discovered through centuries of archaeological excavation. It could reveal the secrets of our universe and hold many secrets that could benefit mankind, cures to diseases that plague this world and predict future events. This is only the tip of the iceberg. The book could hold many secrets that are beyond our imagination."

The discussion was interrupted by a cracking sound. Turning around, they saw Nick and Gagan hurrying towards them. "Chang and his men are in the valley. Switch off all the lanterns."

A few moments passed in complete darkness when a figure appeard in the mouth of the cave. Gagan gripped his axe and headed towards the figure, ready to attack. "Please Stop"! Cried the man throwing his hands in the air and kneeling on the floor. " I am Tsang, Mr.Andrew's friend from Hong Kong." Andy bolted to his feet in amazement. He quickly led Tsang inside the cave. " What on earth are you doing here old chap?" he enquired. " I followed you from Kathmandu Airport to make sure you were in no danger. I gather you have opened the artefact?" " Yes," answered Michael removing the artefact from his backpack. Tsang grabbed the object and examined it closely to everyone surprise. A look of horror came over his face, clenching Andy's shoulder he uttered "This is not the object I hid in your suitcase!"

To be continued…
The Quantum Cypher Book Two:
Fortune Teller Key